★ American Girl

Luciana

BY ERIN TEAGAN

Scholastic Inc.

Published by Scholastic Inc., *Publishers since 1920.* SCHOLASTIC and associated logos are trademarks and/or registered trademarks of Scholastic Inc. The publisher does not have any control over and does not assume any responsibility for author or third-party websites or their content.

This book is a work of fiction. Names, characters, places, and incidents are either the product of the author's imagination or are used fictitiously, and any resemblance to actual persons, living or dead, business establishments, events, or locales is entirely coincidental.

Book design by Suzanne LaGasa
Author photo by Patty Schuchman
Cover and interior illustrations by Lucy Truman

americangirl.com/service

ISBN 978-1-338-18648-2

10 9 8 7 6 5 4 3 2 1   18 19 20 21 22

Printed in the U.S.A.   23 • First printing 2018

FOR JAEDA

CONTENTS

CHAPTER 1

THROUGH THESE DOORS . . .

The first thing I saw was the rocket. From a mile away, it appeared to be pointed straight up into the sky. Dad stopped at the traffic light and slurped his coffee. I bumped my head on the window when we started moving again.

Mom laughed and said, "We'll see it in person in just a minute." She looked at the GPS. "Or forty-five seconds, according to this."

"There's another one!" I shouted. And as we got closer, I saw that there were actually six more rockets, clustered together and standing at attention.

We turned into the parking lot and Mom took out her phone to get a picture of the giant space shuttle that sat just beyond the trees.

"It's the *Pathfinder*," I said. Seeing it gave me goose bumps because all of this was starting to feel real. Going to Space Camp for six days was a dream of mine since as far back as I could remember. "With an external tank, engine nozzles, and two solid rocket boosters," I added, in case they didn't know. My dad was a teacher and my mom was a nurse. They knew a lot about a lot of things, but I was the family expert on space since I was going to be an astronaut.

Someone honked behind us and Dad rolled the car into a parking spot.

Mom unbuckled her seat belt. "What do you think? Are you ready?"

I had read every book on space robots I could find, practiced eating freeze-dried food (even the meatloaf kind), and rode the carnival roller coaster six times in a row to make sure I wouldn't throw up on the space simulators. I was more than ready. I was going to be so good at Space Camp, they might even ask me to be the first girl on Mars.

"Luciana," Mom said, poking me in the shoulder. "Let's go check in."

Dad opened the trunk and took out my rolling suitcase that I'd accidentally filled with all of my space books and drawing pads and colored pencils. Mom pulled out my duffel bag of clothes and my pillow with the solar-system pillowcase.

Even though we were hundreds of miles from Virginia, my stuff still smelled like our house: avocados and coffee and lemon-lime hand soap.

"Wait," I said, pulling everything out of their arms. "I've got this." Astronauts didn't need their parents to carry their stuff, right? Well then, neither did I.

We walked through the red Space Camp gates and then slowly through the shuttle park, and then even more slowly through the rocket park where the *Saturn V* engines towered over us. There was a mass of kids and parents and rolling bags in front of us. I almost dropped my pillow as we walked up to the building to register because there was a sign that said, "Through these doors enter future astronauts, scientists, and engineers." Mom squeezed my shoulder and nudged me ahead.

And then I stopped up the line for a bit because I was too wide to get through the doors with all of my bags and pillows. Dad took my rolling bag—but only because I let him—and then we were inside.

"Name, dear?" asked a lady with a headset.

"Luciana Vega," Mom said, and I gave her a look because astronauts speak for themselves.

"And your age, Luciana?"

"Eleven," I said quickly. "You can call me Luci."

3

"Okay, Luci. You are on Team Odyssey, which is at table seven. You can head over there now," the lady said, moving on to the kid behind me.

I checked out the rest of the campers, some of them taller than me, some of them smaller, almost all of them wearing some kind of space or science clothing. I looked down at my dress that was the colors of the nighttime sky—blue, red, purple, orange. A girl passed me wearing a shooting star headband and another kid squeaked by with rain boots that looked just like an astronaut's moon boots. I could already tell this was my kind of place.

"I wish there had been a camp like this for me when I was growing up," Dad said, taking it all in.

"For math teachers?" Mom said with a laugh.

"Hey, math teachers have dreams too, you know."

We started toward table seven, navigating around display cases full of astronaut gear, flight suits, and helmets. We walked past model rockets and robots and a wall lined with framed pictures of important Space Camp graduates.

"Bet you'll be up there one day," Dad said to me.

"Sure will," Mom agreed.

Except the fancy nameplate on my picture would say, "Luciana Vega, First Girl on Mars."

"Come on, come on," Mom said, urging me past the pictures. "You'll have plenty of time to look at them this week."

When we reached table seven, two people jumped up to shake my hand.

"Good morning, trainee!" they said. "We are your crew trainers. I'm Mallory," the girl said, pointing to herself, "and this is Alex."

Alex waved.

"I'm Luciana," I said.

Mallory clapped her hands. "The essay winner! Right?"

I nodded, my face feeling like it was on fire. I had entered the essay contest for a Space Camp scholarship three years in a row, and this time I had won. Last year, as a consolation, they'd sent me an official Space Camp pen with a light-up solar system, which made me feel like I was on the right track. And that was pretty great.

When I'd found out I was the essay winner, Mom had made her famous *merengue lucuma* cake, a traditional dessert in Chile, and added chocolate chips in the shape of a comet on the top. My favorite.

I shifted the gigantic pillow in my hand to retrieve the folder and name badge Mallory was holding out. "I want to be an astronaut when I grow up."

"Well, your essay on planetary geology was amazing," Alex said, as Mallory nodded in agreement next to him. "You know a lot about space rocks, huh?"

Dad patted me on the back.

"I pretty much know everything about space rocks," I said.

"Is that a purple streak in your hair?" Mallory said. "I love it."

I exchanged looks with Mom, grinning. For the most part my parents didn't mind my colorful ideas, except they probably would have preferred they not be so permanent. A fact I did not realize until after my best friend, Raelyn, and I had already applied the dye to our hair. It was my idea. Kind of a friendship thing with Raelyn back home. She had one to match. A stripe of friendship while we were apart.

Alex laughed. "Well, we need creative future astronauts just like you at Space Camp."

Mallory handed me a backpack. "For all of your Space Camp gear. The girls' bunk is Habitat 4b on the fourth floor. Why don't you head up and get settled and I'll check in once everyone else arrives. Okay?" I fanned my face with the folder, which, after a quick glance, I saw was stuffed with information and maps and schedules.

Mom had to take my pillow so I could get up the stairs without causing another backup. When we reached my floor, I felt like I was in some kind of movie, floating in a space station far above Earth. The walls were metal and curved. We stopped in front of Habitat 4b, and I brushed my hand along the wall. The shiny silver was cold to the touch. I took out my name badge, waved it in front of the lock, and we went inside.

The inside of the sleep station was white, just like I'd imagine a space habitat to be, including the bunk beds, a long desktop, and a small bank of lockers. Mom checked her watch for the time and gave Dad a look. They had to leave for the airport soon. I took a breath. Even though Space Camp was my kind of place, I wished my parents didn't have to rush off so fast.

"Are you okay, sweetie?" Mom asked.

"Are you kidding? I'm at Space Camp!" I said, bouncing onto a bed. But my body throbbed with nerves. What if I had a catastrophic crisis or an ear infection or something? Mom and Dad would be a few states away.

Mom sat next to me. "If we hear anything about Isadora, we'll call you right away, okay?"

My stomach fluttered. Baby Isadora. I was already calling her *hermanita* in my head. Little sister.

"Promise?" I said.

Dad kissed me on the forehead. "Promise. They should have received our paperwork by now. We expect to hear something any day."

Baby Isadora was at an orphanage in Chile that Mom and Dad had visited a few months ago. Sometimes they went back to Chile, where they grew up, to help in the hospitals and orphanages and to visit Abuelita, my grandma, and the rest of our family. Mom and Dad fell in love with Isadora, a baby who clutched a stuffed penguin. After they got home and we talked about it, we decided to adopt her. The orphanage just had to accept us first.

"Okay," I said. "I hope it doesn't take too long."

It was pretty much what I had wanted my whole life. A baby sister.

"Well," Mom said, snapping me out of my thoughts, digging in her purse. "I thought you might need this." She pulled out a necklace. It was my star. Polished and shining. My parents had bought it for me on my first birthday and I only wore it for special occasions.

Mom kissed me on top of the head. "Your first sleepaway camp is the most special kind of occasion."

"We're proud of you, Luciana," Dad added.

And then after a long hug and a thousand more kisses, they were gone.

CHAPTER 2

ROOMMATES

At first all I could do was sit on my bunk bed, holding my star necklace. What if I wasn't ready for Space Camp? I mean, I was only eleven. Maybe I needed my parents to carry my pillows and space books sometimes. And maybe I wasn't ready to sleep in a bunk called a habitat with four strangers. What if I couldn't find the bathroom? What if—

I shook my head. I was Luci Vega. Raelyn would tell me to stop being ridiculous. She'd tell me that if I wanted to be the first girl on Mars, I'd deal with way worse stuff than saying good-bye to my parents for a few days. She'd tell me this was the place to show everyone that I had what it took to be an astronaut.

Something on the wall caught my eye. A framed picture of Sally Ride hung above the desks. The first American woman in space. When NASA still had the space shuttle program, she controlled a giant robotic arm hundreds of miles above Earth, and here I was, worried about missing my parents. I hopped off my bed, stood up, and marched over to my bag, unpacking my drawing pads and pencils and then every science book I brought: *Science, the Stars, and You*; *Rocket Science 101*; *Robotics Is for Girls!*; and my favorite, *You Can Be an Astronaut Too!*

I opened my duffel bag and dumped my T-shirts, my favorite pajamas from the planetarium, and my emoji toothbrush that was the same as Raelyn's into a locker, shutting it tight. And then I grabbed my sketch pad and favorite purple and red and green pencils, which were only just nubs at this point, and climbed back onto my bunk bed to draw while I waited for the rest of my bunkmates.

And then I remembered: There on my bed was the backpack from check-in. I pulled the drawstrings open and when I looked inside, my heart thumped double-time. Because right there, folded up nice and neat, was an official Space Camp flight suit. I pulled it out and pressed it against my body. Walking over to the mirror, I almost teared up because: Was it just me or did I look a little bit like Sally Ride?

There was a commotion in the hall and I barely had

the chance to pretend I wasn't admiring myself when the habitat door burst open.

"I call top bunk!" a little girl shouted, hurling herself at the closest bunk-bed ladder.

And then it felt like fifty more people poured into the room, little kids and bigger kids, girls and boys, moms and dads, and maybe even a grandma or two. And was that a dog?

"Someone shut that door so Pepper doesn't get out!" a lady shouted. A little dog popped up out of a purse and hurled itself onto the tile floor, tip-tapping all around.

He sniffed my fuzzy star slippers and when I reached down to pet him, he licked my hand. This guy was probably half the size of Rae's bunny back home, although his ears were probably twice the size of his tiny body.

When I looked up again, the dog had trotted away, but there was a girl standing kind of frozen in the middle of the room. I waved and smiled. There were also two little girls hanging over the safety bars on the top bunks, a couple of boys playing hide-and-seek in the lockers, and a mixture of adults and kids wrestling and bumping into the desks.

I put my drawing pad down and got off my bed just as another girl was heaving a pillow and blanket onto the bed above mine.

"I'm Luciana," I said, helping her push her blanket all the way onto her bed. "You can call me Luci."

"I'm Ella. That's my sister, Meg," she said pointing to the now slightly unfrozen girl I had spotted in the middle of the room.

Meg and Ella looked like sisters with freckled noses and the same dark hair. Except Meg's was pulled into a bouncy ponytail and Ella's was pin-straight and down her back.

Meg clutched a lady around her waist, probably her mom. I waved again, but Meg's face remained serious.

"She's only nine. This is her first sleepaway camp, and that's my cousin Charlotte," Ella said, pointing to another girl trying to pry Meg away from her mom.

"Wow," I said, thinking about how nervous I'd felt saying good-bye to my parents, and I was a whole two years older than Meg. "That's very brave."

"Come on, Meg," Charlotte said. "It's going to be so fun. Like we're real astronauts, okay? Did you bring your flashlights?"

Meg nodded.

"And like a thousand glow sticks," Ella said, walking over to them. "Hope you don't need a totally dark room to sleep," she said, turning back to me.

I shrugged and inspected a suspicious puddle by my desk. "I'm okay with a thousand glow sticks."

"Bring it in!" one of the dads yelled, and everyone huddled in the center of the room for a group hug. One of the moms pulled me in and I was shoulder to shoulder with a group of strangers and there was lots of kissing on foreheads and squeezing one another hard and reminding everyone that family was everything.

And then the huddle was over and moms and dads peeled kids out of top bunks and out of desk chairs and swabbed up puddles and collected shoes and bubble gum wrappers. There were more hugs and even some sniffles and then all at once, they were gone and the room was silent, except for the buzzing in my ears.

Ella, Charlotte, and Meg looked at me. "Sorry about that," Charlotte said.

"Are you all from the same family?" I asked. Secretly I wished my parents could adopt fifty Isadoras so we'd be one giant family like that. Most of my family was back in Chile and I hardly ever got to see them.

Meg nodded. "All the cousins are on spring break." She looked at the door, still a little sniffly, and Ella gave her a hug.

"My brother is twelve. He's doing the Aviation Challenge camp," Charlotte explained. "And my older sister is sixteen and she came to Space Camp when she was eleven like me and maybe even stayed in this same bunk." She took a big breath, pushing a sparkly headband back through her curly hair. Even though her hair was much lighter than her cousins', she had their greenish-hazel eyes.

"Everyone else is too little so they're going to the beach with the aunts and uncles. How many kids in your family?" Ella asked me.

"Just me." I sighed. I mean, it was nice that everyone had their own spot on the couch and seat at the table. And never once had I found a plastic spider under my pillow, which from what I'd heard, happened a lot around little brothers. But sometimes it was too echoey-quiet in my house, especially when Mom had an emergency and had to work late. Which happened a lot.

"Wow, I can't even imagine that," Charlotte said. "My mom makes me share socks with my brother and sometimes ice-cream sandwiches at the pool and—"

"Do you have purple hair?" Meg said, reaching out to touch my purple streak.

"My best friend and I did it together," I said, nodding.

Meg grinned. "That is so cool—"

"Don't even think about it," Ella said, swatting her hand away.

Another girl appeared in the doorway. She let her heavy bag slide off her shoulder and thump to the floor.

"Hallo!" she said in a thick accent. "I'm Johanna. From Germany." She had wavy bright blonde hair that barely touched her shoulders, pulled back with a bobby pin. She dragged her duffel bag across the floor.

"Goodness!" Charlotte said. "What do you have in there?"

"Books," Johanna said. "Lots of books."

I straightened. "Really? I brought my books too."

"Are they about mechanical engineering and electrical circuits?"

"Not specifically," I said, laughing, "but that sounds interesting."

Meg flung herself onto her bed and dumped out an assortment of flashlights and glow sticks and a stuffed animal dog that looked a lot like Pepper.

Charlotte took her flight suit from her bag. "Guys, look." She put it on her bed and then I remembered what I had in my bag.

"Does anyone want to put their name on their suit?" I asked, pulling out a bunch of glitter stickers. "I brought enough for everyone."

Meg sprang herself off her bed, rushing over. "Me! Me!"

Johanna and Meg and Charlotte swarmed over my sticker sheets.

"Should we put them on the front, like right here?" I pointed to the chest pocket. "Or on the back like here?"

"Wait. Stop." Ella climbed off her top bunk. "This probably isn't even allowed."

Meg froze, a glitter letter *M* dangling from the tip of a finger. "Why not?"

"We're at Space Camp, Meg. I'm just saying. It will look unprofessional."

"Oh," I said. "It's probably not against the rules." Although I wasn't completely positive. "Also it will look nice and the good thing is nobody will forget us!"

The room got kind of silent and serious and Ella was giving all sorts of stern looks to Meg and Charlotte.

Johanna stuck a golden *J* onto her flight suit and held it up. *"Das ist Spitze!"* she bellowed, breaking the silence. And then she smiled. "I mean . . . uh, awesome!"

And then we all burst out laughing, everyone trying to say what Johanna had just said, but failing horribly.

I held out an orange glitter *E* for Ella, and for a moment, I thought she was going to take it and join my glitter letter party.

"Be nice," Charlotte said to Ella under her breath.

But instead Ella shook her head and walked past me, folding up her flight suit neat and tidy and putting it in her locker.

CHAPTER 3

MISSION CONTROL CENTER

Everyone was pretty much finished unpacking, except for Charlotte, who'd brought about a million things too many, when there was a knock.

I hopped off my bed, dodging Ella's swinging legs, and opened the door. Something lit up in disco lights and rolled over my feet before I could move out of the way. It was a little white robot dog with long ears and a wagging stub of a tail.

"Aw!" Meg said, running over. "He is the cu-test!"

The dog barked and spun in a circle. "BARK. BARK."

"What do you think of our mascot?" Mallory said from the doorway.

"Did you design him yourself?" Johanna asked, kneeling on the floor for a better look. The robot wheeled over to her. "Is that a touch sensor? Is he rechargeable?"

"Wow. I've never seen a dog like that or a robot like that and did you make that at camp?" Charlotte asked.

"I made him my first week as a Space Camp crew trainer," Mallory said. "And, yes, I designed him myself. His name is Orion."

Orion stood up on two legs. "BARK."

"He's telling you it's time to meet the rest of Team Odyssey and perform our first mission training. An E-V-A practice."

"An E-V-what?" Charlotte asked.

"An extravehicular activity," Ella said.

"Otherwise known as a space walk," Mallory said, leading Orion into the hallway.

With that, everyone put on their flight suits and straightened their beds, a Space Camp rule according to Ella, who had read the entire rules and regulations booklet we'd received in our orientation packets a few weeks ago. And maybe memorized them.

Everyone grabbed their Space Camp backpacks and followed Orion down the hallway. We went through the habitat common area where they were streaming news from the International Space Station, past a hall of artifacts and a Space Camp store, and out the front doors.

"Shortcut across the shuttle park," Mallory called over her shoulder.

"*Beeindruckend!*" Johanna shouted. "I mean, wow!" Charlotte and Meg were way ahead, racing Orion down the sidewalk, Mallory and Ella hollering at them to slow down. "We're going to walk right under the *Pathfinder.*"

But there was no stopping and staring this time around. Meg and Charlotte were already at the door on the other side, waiting impatiently for the rest of us to catch up. Orion zipped along beside us.

When we got inside, we walked past the dining hall and stopped at a sign that said, "MISSION CONTROL CENTER," where the boys' bunk—the other half of Team Odyssey—waited, everyone dressed in flight suits.

One boy thrust his hand out to me. He said, "My name is James and I'll be your commander for this mission." After looking at my glitter name, he added, "Luciana."

Alex put his hand on James's shoulder. "There are no commanders on this mission, trainee."

James grinned and raised his eyebrows at him. "You sure? Because I happen to be the best at commanding things." He was tall with his hair cut close to his head, almost like he was a real-life commander in the navy or something.

"We're sure," Ella said, barging into the conversation. She crossed her arms, refusing to shake his hand.

Charlotte tugged on Ella's flight suit. "Be nice."

"Oh! Oh!" Meg said, bouncing on the balls of her feet. "Can I be commander?"

Ella rolled her eyes.

Mallory and Alex pushed through the swingy hatch doors into the mission control area and led us inside. "No commanders for this mission," Alex repeated.

Johanna stopped in front of me and I ran into her. And then I saw what made basically the entire group, boys and girls, commanders and noncommanders, stop in their tracks.

"Welcome to the mission floor," Mallory said.

There were spacecrafts and space habitats and greenhouses growing leafy plants in hydroponic gardens, not to mention a black sky ceiling with twinkling star lights. It was like all of a sudden something was in my eyes and I had to blink fast to stop them from overflowing. I held my star necklace and made a wish on the biggest star I saw. *Please let me be a real astronaut one day. Please let me be the first girl on Mars.*

"Wow," Meg whispered. "Are we, like, really in space or something?"

Johanna grinned. "Cool."

"This way," Mallory said, motioning to a rack lined with space suits. "Suit up!"

I walked up to the nearest space suit, just hanging there, waiting for an astronaut to step inside. An astronaut like me, maybe.

"Lower torso assembly goes on first," Alex explained, holding up a pair of overalls that looked a lot like snow pants. "Then boots, then upper torso assembly." He pointed to a jacket that looked more like football pads. "And then, the helmet and gloves."

I helped Johanna balance herself while she pulled on her astronaut pants and stepped into her boots.

"In the logbook, it says these suits in real life can weigh almost three hundred pounds or something," Ella lectured. Of course, in space they weigh nothing at all.

The Space Camp logbook had been in our bags with our flight suits. Mine was zipped into one of my suit pockets and I was happy to see that there were a bunch of pages at the back to make observations. Or drawings.

"How did you read that already?" I asked.

Ella glared at me. "Maybe reading the logbook would have been a better use of your time than putting sparkly stickers all over the place," she said disapprovingly.

"Oh," I said, backing up in surprise. Because she was making it very hard to be friends with her. And it was practically camp law to be friends with your bunkmates.

"Ella," Charlotte said, pulling her pants tighter. "Stop it."

"And anyway these suits aren't completely accurate because we'd have to wear a layer of cooling clothing so we didn't burn up in the heat of the heavy suits," Ella continued like she hadn't just been so mean. I patted down my glitter letter *L* on my flight suit, which was already starting to peel up.

Johanna lurched forward, nearly fully assembled, and Charlotte and I caught her. Mallory handed me a lower torso assembly and I put it on, hiking my suspenders up and sliding into a pair of moon boots. Lunar overshoes, according to the logbook, or at least according to Ella.

James flipped his visor up, already in his astronaut

gear. "In case you didn't know, it's not even hot in space all the time."

Ella turned to him, also all the way dressed, and it was like an astronaut face-off. "I was going to say that. Or they could have a layer to protect them from cold."

Orion circled Johanna and me, and then Meg stomped by like a zombie abominable snowman with her arms out for balance. Except it didn't work and she tumbled onto the floor, losing a glove that was obviously too big, and a boot too.

Ella broke her standoff with James and rushed over to help her up.

"Meg is just like my little sister," Johanna said to me, pausing while she put a glove on. "She's eight and she dreams of coming here too."

"I don't have a little sister, but I'm getting one soon." I grabbed a helmet from a stack of cubes on the wall. "Is it hard being a big sister?"

"Sometimes," she said, struggling with her other glove. "Like if she steals your favorite shirt and puts paint all over it." She smiled at me. "But your sister probably won't do that."

I pictured me and Isadora riding our bikes around the block, picking mulberries off the tree in our yard, and making sidewalk-chalk cities. I'd tell her my favorite folktale from Chile about the sun and moon. I'd let her borrow my digital microscope. I looked back up at the biggest star and made another wish. For a sister. For Isadora to come home.

"Let's get you into a suit that fits," Mallory said, taking Meg by the hand.

"The rest of you can follow me," Alex said, bringing us all to the main part of the mission area. "For this simulation, you're a team of astronauts on the ISS, otherwise known as the International Space Station." He led us to the biggest module on the mission floor, an exact replica of the real ISS.

"Your mission is to replace various tiles on the outside of the ISS as part of a materials experiment."

"The MISSE," Ella added, something else she probably learned from her logbook reading.

James straightened. "Materials International Space Station Experiment."

"I know that," Ella retorted. "MISSE is the acronym."

Charlotte was walking with Johanna and she rolled her eyes. "It's going to be a long week with those two."

Alex continued. "A real concern for astronauts doing an EVA . . ."

"That's an extravehicular activity," Ella announced, even though I'm pretty sure most of us knew that. Especially since Mallory had already told us girls back in our sleep station.

Alex shot her a warning look and started again. "The oxygen levels are built into your suits and are carefully controlled. A real concern during an EVA is getting a tear in your suit, or snagging your suit, which leaves a small hole. If this happens, the suit will lose pressurization. You'll have approximately five minutes before your oxygen reaches dangerous levels and you will have to return to the spacecraft."

Meg ran by again, catching up with Ella, this time managing to stay upright.

Mallory stopped us in front of the ISS and pointed to two metal trays embedded in the side of the spacecraft. "The purpose of the experiment is to test different materials to see how they perform in space with all the UV radiation and exposure to extreme temperatures.

Your job is to take ten new material tiles"—she opened one of the metal-toolbox-looking containers on a tall table in between the two metal trays on the ISS—"and find each tile's correct place on the tray." She pulled out a metal tile with a bunch of switches on it and fit it into a rectangular spot on the metal tray. And then she pulled out a different tile, this one full of wires and shaped like a triangle, and measured it up against a few places on the tray until she found where it would go. "After you're sure of the fit, secure each tile with this adhesive foam." She held up a canister with a spray nozzle.

"It's like a puzzle," Meg said, nodding.

"Exactly," Mallory said, smiling. "A space puzzle."

"You'll go two at a time," Alex added. "And the two trainees who perform their EVA with the fewest errors in five minutes will get to captain a robotics team."

I could see Ella and James at the front of the pack, both of their heads swinging to attention.

"My robotics team at home basically wins every competition every single year," James declared.

Ella perked up. "My team went to state last year."

"But you lost then, right, Ella?" Meg said. "I remember that. You were so mad, you cr—"

Ella gave her a look that could have melted a Mars glacier. "We would have won, actually," she said through gritted teeth, "if it weren't for a faulty charging station. Our robot ran out of juice right in the middle of the competition."

"Rookie mistake," James whispered to his bunkmates, and Ella looked like she was about to erupt.

My belly was starting to turn. I hadn't expected there to be so many genius kids here. I patted my astronaut suit, feeling my star necklace underneath. Did they all want to be astronauts like I did?

Mallory shushed Ella and James's bickering and led us to the International Space Station. I took a deep breath and climbed the three metal stairs to go inside.

As I looked around, my heart skipped a beat. The inside of the module looked and felt like how I'd imagined the real thing would be. Buttons and switches and screens flashing data. The walls were lined with cabinets in all different sizes, closed and latched tight. There were computer stations and places to run experiments. Everything was clean and white.

"There's an astronaut toilet," Noah from the boys' bunk snorted.

We all sat in a circle in the node of the space station, and when we looked up, there was even a cupula, a giant window that gave a view of the night sky.

Alex appeared with a clipboard. "Johanna and Tanner. You're up first." A boy hopped up on the other side of James, and he joined Johanna at the door. They left with a wave and a thumbs-up and we were alone, all of us sitting in our hot space suits on the floor, waiting for our turns.

"There is a lot of waiting for astronauts in real life as well," Mallory said, leaning against the far wall. "Patience is key. In fact, Japanese astronauts are required to fold one thousand paper cranes during their training. If I were you, I'd take this time to make notes and reread the section about this activity in the logbook."

"Well, I'm not one for waiting," Ella announced. "I'm more for *doing*."

"Ella doesn't like to lose at things," Meg whispered to me. "In case you couldn't tell."

I didn't like losing either. And if we were being honest, it was probably my least favorite thing if you didn't count centipedes. The big hairy kind at least.

"Especially now since she doesn't have any friends left," Meg said.

"What?" I said.

Johanna and Tanner came back. "Just two errors," Johanna said, spacesuit-less and grinning.

"You get to hang from the ceiling!" Tanner said.

"Meg and José. You're up next," Alex said.

Meg stood up so fast, she teetered in her moon boots for a moment before gaining her balance. And then she strode out of the room like she was the queen of space and I didn't even get to ask her about the Ella-having-no-friends thing.

CHAPTER 4

SPACE WALK

James and I were called last. Johanna and Charlotte smiled at me and I knew they felt a little bad that I got stuck with Mr. Know-It-All-King-of-Robotics. James sighed like all of this was everyday boring stuff, but when we left the space station and the entire mission floor came into view, I heard him gasp a little through the headset in my helmet. He squinted his eyes at me when he caught me looking at him.

"I've never seen an astronaut with purple hair before," he said.

I pulled up my visor, sweating inside my suit. "Astronauts come with hair in all shapes and sizes and colors, James."

He snorted. "That's the kind of stuff your mom has to tell you. It's like mom law."

I ignored his comments and focused on Alex, who was standing next to two harnesses attached to the twinkly ceiling. The room was quiet and dark with blue lights illuminating the mission area. "Step on in," he said.

James quickly grabbed his harness and just as quickly got his boots stuck in the legholes. I took my time and slid each leg through the harness, and by the time James untangled himself, I was swinging midair above him. Smiling, because I couldn't help it. Obviously, he didn't think the girl with the purple stripe in her hair had the skills to be a good astronaut. I was going to have to show him.

Even though I was only a few feet from the ground, it felt like I was miles above the earth. Was this how it felt to be on a real space walk? Because if so, I wanted to go on a real space walk every day of my whole life.

But right now, I needed to concentrate on the challenge. In front of me was the metal materials tray, stuck to the side of the ISS. Next to me on the tall table sat two toolboxes, one for me and one for James, each with its own material tiles and a canister of adhesive foam. James zipped up to his materials tray and supplies across from me.

"Ready to begin?" Alex asked, looking at a stopwatch, and we nodded our heads through our astronaut helmets. "Okay, ten tiles, go!"

I threw open my box of tiles, taking them all out and laying them on my side of the table.

I eyed the tiles, looking for the right ones to fit the board. There were tiles made of plastic and metal in all different thicknesses, tiles with hooks on them, wires, or switches, even a tile that looked like glass but felt like clear, hard plastic.

"Don't forget that you're supposed to be in a microgravity environment now," Alex warned from where he stood right under us. He reached up and grabbed one of my tiles.

"Hey," I said. "I need that one."

"Microgravity," he repeated, grabbing two more tiles. "Don't forget, nothing would stay in place."

I rushed to collect the rest of my supply before Alex could take more, bumping into the ISS and sending one of James's tiles back to the floor.

"Watch out!" James yelled.

With one hand holding me steady, I assessed my tiles again, way behind James who was working methodically through the challenge.

"Did you even read the directions in the logbook?" he said.

I ignored him. And no, I hadn't, if we were being honest.

It was nearly impossible to grab anything out of my supply box while wearing the giant gloves. I changed my strategy and took it slow, taking out one tile at a time and finding its place on the board. It was even more difficult squirting a dollop of foam onto the metal tray before fixing the tile into place, but soon I got a good system down and I picked up my pace.

It was hard work and even harder being so sweaty-hot and floating all over the place in my harness. I pulled out another tile, not even looking at the size, and measured it up against the spots on my tray. It would fit the one all the way in the corner. The hardest one to reach.

"That's one minute already," Alex said.

I pulled my body across the tray, holding the foam under my arm and the tile in my hand. With my free hand, I squirted a bit of foam and pushed the tile into place. Seven more to go. I stuffed the foam back under an arm and pulled out another tile, making sure to shut the top of the box tight so nothing floated away. I was finally making good progress when James dropped his foam.

"Oh no," he said through the headset.

Not to mention he only had placed five tiles.

"Two minutes," Alex said.

I handed James my foam. "Use it and pass it back."

He looked surprised but then grabbed it without wasting any more time. And, actually, it was easier for me to retrieve a tile and find its place on the tray without being afraid I'd lose the foam dispenser from under my arm.

"Foam, please," I said, and James handed it back.

And then when I was finished, I handed it back to him, and we repeated the process until I had placed all of my tiles and I didn't need it back again.

"Time!" Alex called, clicking his stopwatch.

"You placed all your tiles, Luciana. Well done." He grinned and gave me a thumbs-up.

"Yes!" I tried giving him two thumbs-up because I was doubly excited at my time, but my body swung out of control and I crashed into the ISS again.

Alex laughed and pulled me down.

"Finished! Got them all in, too," I heard James say through my headset as I tore off my space suit.

"Looks like we have our team captains," Alex said.

James gave me a high five when he got back to the

ground, my bare hand to his gloved hand. "Thanks for helping me up there."

"Sure," I said, surprised again because this didn't seem like the same James who had been fighting with Ella all afternoon.

"Hope you're as good at building robots as you are putting tiles onto a metal tray." He kicked off his lunar overshoes.

"Sure am," I said, even though I wasn't totally sure I was so good at building robots. I had only built one or two before. For fun. With Raelyn.

James pulled off his helmet, smirking. "Doubt it."

And the James from before was back.

"You'll see," I said, and then I walked off, leaving him there.

CHAPTER 5

RED ROVERS

Before dinner, James and I—the official captains—picked our teams. There were six teams in our age bracket participating in the robotics challenge at Space Camp and according to Alex and Mallory, competition was going to be fierce.

"I'm glad our team is just everyone in our sleeping station," Meg said, popping a meatball into her mouth.

I eyed James and his team across the dining hall. Noah adjusted his glasses and stuck his tongue out at me.

"I'm just glad James is not on my team," I said, and Ella groaned.

"Bunk versus bunk is so stupid," she said, the sandwich in front of her untouched. She probably wanted to be on James's team so they could form some kind of super-robotics squad. "Did you even read about the robotics competition in the orientation packet they sent us?"

I had not.

"Because there are a lot of rules and also details that a captain should know about and—"

"Ella. Stop," Charlotte said.

But she didn't stop. "What about the bolt system, do you know how that works? Do you know that you have to earn bolts to even build a robot? And what about sponsorships? Do you know about those? And—ow!"

"Sorry," Charlotte said. "You deserved that pinch. Luci is captain and I think she'll do a great job and you just need to stop it, please."

My heart was pounding because, pretty much, I didn't know all of those things that Ella was talking about. The orientation stuff was still on my desk at home. Barely touched.

"We need a team name," Meg said, slurping her star soup. "Something like the Sparkle Unicorns"—she wiped soup off her face—"or the Space Kittens?" She bounced in her seat. "And we can all put purple stripes in our hair!"

"That would be so cool," I said, ignoring Ella's grimace. "What about Glitter and Gears?"

Johanna ran up to the table with her second helping. "I think we have this in Germany, *käse Spätzle*? Little tubey things with cheesy sauce all over them?"

"Macaroni and cheese?" Meg said.

"Yes, yes. Macaroni and cheese!" She squeezed in next to me and took a big forkful.

"I really like all your ideas way better than my sister's team name, which was the Sprinkled Donuts." Charlotte bit into a French fry. "That was her favorite food by the way, and my favorite food is chicken pot pie but no way do I want chicken in our team name."

"My soccer team in Germany is called the Wild Cats," Johanna said. "I kind of like that name."

Ella sighed. "That has nothing to do with science."

"How about the Red Rovers?" Charlotte said.

"Oh! Like the game and also like the red planet!" I said. "I love it!"

"That's the best one," Johanna agreed, with a fork pointed at Charlotte.

"What about Team Robotics?" Ella suggested, playing with the little flag toothpick of a rocket in her turkey sandwich. "Clear and simple."

"Okay. We have a lot of good names. Let's vote," I said, proud of myself for sounding like such a great captain. See? You didn't have to read a thousand pamphlets to be a good leader. "Raise your hand for Sparkle Unicorns." Nobody raised her hand.

Meg blew air out of her mouth. "Figures. Nobody ever likes my ideas."

"Space Kittens?" I said and Meg raised her hand. "Glitter and Gears?" No takers. "Wild Cats?" Not even Johanna raised her hand. "Red Rovers?" Three hands popped up. "And, lastly, Team Robotics." Ella raised her hand.

Charlotte clapped and stood up because it was obvious her team name, Red Rovers, was the winner.

Ella snapped her rocket toothpick in half and Charlotte looked at her with disapproval, taking the jagged pieces away from her. I glanced at Meg, remembering what she'd said about Ella not having any friends, and even though Ella wasn't the most pleasant person in the world, it made me feel a little sad for her.

After dinner, we headed to the robotics lab, on the first level in the same building, not too far from the crew galley. We could see it from way down the hall, Orion leading the way, the oversized red plastic brick walls separating the lab from the rest of Space Camp. Over the door was a row of framed pictures of previous winning robotics teams holding up patches that said "Best Rover." I stopped for a good look, because it was like a wall of fame just for the robotics lab. And maybe it wasn't the same as getting on the wall in the common area with all the real-life astronauts who used to be Space Campers, but it was still a wall of fame. And I wanted to be on it.

Johanna pulled me into the lab and we all took a seat, Ella at the tip-top of the table like she was in charge. And to make matters worse, we shared our lab time with James's team, the RoboEngineers. The other four teams met at different times during the day.

"Welcome to the Space Camp Robotics Lab," a guy with a white lab coat said. "I am Leo, your robotics crew trainer."

"What's that?" James interrupted, pointing to a sensor high up on a shelf, sitting on top of a minipodium made out of building bricks. There was a tag hanging off it that said, "10,000,000 BOLTS."

Leo smiled. "That is the coveted gyro sensor. The most expensive part in the lab and also probably the most valuable for our competition table."

"How do we get it?" James asked, and Ella rolled her eyes.

"You need to earn it," Leo said with a smile. "I'll get to that in a bit."

"Why do we want that?" I whispered to Johanna.

"It's for a balancing robot," Johanna whispered back. "Like, you could make a robot with one wheel and it wouldn't tip over."

Leo moved in front of a big square table in the middle of the room. It was a tournament table for a robot competition, which I knew from looking over Ella's shoulder as she'd read her logbook while standing in line for the bathroom. "This is the table we'll use in the competition on Thursday. You'll have all week to build your robot."

I scanned the table and took note of everything our robot would have to work with, around, or through: a mountain made out of dust and rocks, something that looked like a space tower, and a bunch of colored balls rolling around. In the middle was a flag that said, "MARS MISSION 2.0."

"This is the scenario: You are a team of astronauts who have been selected to go to Mars, but you'll need to build a capable rover to go with you. Your rover must take a Mars rock sample and place it in a Mars Ascent Vehicle for launch to orbit. There are four stages." Leo pointed to the balls rolling around on the table. "First, identify the sample, which in this competition will be the red rocks only, or the red balls." He picked a ball up and threw it to James. He caught it perfectly, of course. "Second stage is to collect the ball, third stage is to break the ball open and retrieve the smaller sample inside." He squeezed the ball hard, cracking it open and pulling out a marble. "Last and final stage is to bring your sample to the space elevator and send it into orbit, where it will be picked up by a capsule at a later date." The elevator sat at the top of the dirt mountain and was made out of building bricks. I could see why you needed a robot that wouldn't tip over.

"How do you win?" Noah asked.

"Did anyone read the orientation material?" Ella sighed. "The team with the most bolts at the end of the competition wins."

"Thank you, Miss," Leo said to Ella. "Are you all familiar with the bolt system?" Everyone nodded their heads except for me. "It's our point system. On Thursday, your robots will be judged by how many stations they complete on the table and how fast. The more stations your robot completes in the least time, the more bolts you'll earn."

Leo clapped his hands. "The catch is that each part you use on your robot costs bolts. So, in order to build a supercool robot for the competition, you have to first earn bolts. You can do this in two ways." He held up a finger. "One: Complete the daily lab challenges for bolts." He held up a second finger. "Two: Find a sponsor."

"What are sponsors?" I whispered to Johanna, supersecret so Ella didn't hear, but Johanna was too busy reading the challenge for the day on the board to answer.

"Today your challenge is to build a simple rover that responds to a remote control by moving forward, backward, and in a circle," Leo said. "No programming required. Just a basic exercise to get you started in the lab."

"I could make that robot in my sleep," James said to his team.

Ella stood up, glaring at James. "Can we start already?"

Leo laughed, glancing at Mallory and Alex, who, if you asked me, were looking pretty exhausted over the Ella and James situation.

"Today's challenge is worth one million bolts. If you need a refresher of the rules, check out the poster on the wall by the rover parts; otherwise, go ahead and get started."

James and Ella fast-walked to the parts wall, elbowing each other.

"Hmph," Charlotte said. "What's a robot without programming?"

"We'll need an infrared sensor to link to a remote control," Johanna said, mostly talking to herself and shuffling over to the parts wall.

"Can we make a puppy like Orion?" Meg asked.

Ella came back to the table with a few parts she had collected. "No, Meg. We have to keep it simple."

"Infrared sensor!" Johanna was back at our table, waving the sensor around.

"Great," Ella said, grabbing it. "This is all we really need." She spread out the parts in front of us, and my stomach tightened because I was basically letting her take this whole thing over. "What do you guys think? Clean and simple."

The rest of the team nodded, already building.

"Kind of boring, though," I said, and that's when I got my idea.

I left the team to explore the robot parts in the bins along the wall—building bricks, beams, connectors, and axles to make wheel sets—looking for just the right part. In the last container, on the very bottom of the wall of parts, there was a bin of LED lights. I was an expert at making things with LED lights because we made light-up bracelets last summer in Maker Camp. I grabbed a bunch of bricks, some lights, and a battery. I couldn't wait to surprise the rest of the Red Rovers.

I was still building when the teams started lining up to show off their creations. Everyone's looked the same, pretty much. Four wheels attached to a battery pack attached to an infrared sensor that would make it run by remote control. Boring. Boring. Boring. I ran to join my team just as Ella placed our rover in the taped-off arena on the floor.

"Wait!" I said, and I attached my part to the top of the robot and turned on the battery. "RED ROVERS" lit up in neon LED lights, flashing and pulsing.

"Ohhhhhhh," Meg said.

"*Spitze!*" Johanna said, which I remembered meant *awesome*.

"No!" Ella said, and she tried to grab the rover back from the floor, but it was too late. Meg pressed the remote control and it raced off. I mean, was Ella trying to destroy my creation? In case she didn't know, it was more than just her on this team. Anyway she'd thank me later when we won a thousand-million bolts for creative thinking.

"They deduct bolts based on the weight of your rover, Luciana," Ella said, "not to mention each part has a cost too." And our team kind of got silent, all except for Meg, who was showing the rest of the groups how well our rover spun and rolled backward.

"Weight?" I said, panic filling my stomach.

"Did you even read about the bolt system for challenge robots like they told us to?" Ella said, her face red. "Did you even ask the rest of the team?"

Charlotte stepped between us. "Ella. It's okay, guys. It was just a mistake."

But it was more than just a mistake, and based on the look on my teammates' faces, they knew it too. Just the battery alone weighed almost as much as the rest of the robot. What had I done? Why hadn't I just taken a second to read the directions over by the part wall?

Ella fumed. "How are we going to afford to buy parts for the competition robot now?"

Charlotte tried to calm her down. "It's okay. We'll earn a bunch of bolts over the week. We'll make it up."

But when we weighed our robot, it became obvious that it was going to take more than just a bunch of bolts. Because at the end of it, even though our robot did great at the challenge, we were still at negative two million bolts. The Red Rovers were in last place, by a lot, all thanks to me.

CHAPTER 6

SPONSORS

That night, everyone met in the habitat common area to watch a movie about Jupiter. I just kind of stood there while the rest of my team picked out some cushions and took a seat on the floor, nobody really talking.

Except for Charlotte. She talked for all of us. ". . . and then my sister was in the hall where they keep the stuffed monkeys and all of the lights went out, like—*BAM!*—complete and total darkness and if it hadn't been for her really good sense of direction, my sister would have never made it out of Space Camp alive and—"

"That hall that is very dark and creepy?" Meg said, checking behind her. "Stuffed monkeys?"

"Yes, like this—" And Charlotte did an impression of the stuffed monkeys she was talking about. "Also I'm pretty sure the real and actual grave of one of the original monkeys in space is here."

Meg stood up. "Like right here in this very spot?"

"No," Ella said. "That's a lie. There are no stuffed monkeys, Charlotte, and also they planted a garden in the monkeys' memory."

"I know," Charlotte said, whispering, "because they stuffed the body and put it in there." She pointed down the dark hallway of artifacts on the other side of the room.

"Actually," Charlotte continued. "Miss Baker, one of the Monkeynauts who flew in space, lived at the Rocket Center until she was twenty-six. She is buried on the grounds of the center."

Meg whimpered and grabbed Ella.

"It's not true, Meg, there are no monkeys anywhere at Space Camp."

"Or are there?" Charlotte said, grinning.

James kept looking over at us and smirking until I finally blew the hair out of my face and said, "WHAT?"

"Oh, me?" He looked around like he had no idea I was talking to him. "I just hope you guys weren't planning on buying the gyro sensor, because we already have five million bolts."

Ella stood back up. "Your score was less than one million bolts after they weighed your robot from the challenge."

"Oh," James said, smiling. "That was before we got sponsored."

"Sponsored?" I said.

The lights dimmed and kids settled onto their pillows, the movie just about to start.

"Sponsored," James repeated like he was bored. "It's when someone on the staff really likes your robot idea and they give you a bunch of bolts—"

"We know what it means, thank you very much," Ella said, even though he was talking to me. "Who in their right mind would sponsor a team like yours?"

"Ella," Charlotte said, quietly. "Be nice. Sit down."

The movie started with a crash of music and a close-up of the planet Jupiter, making us all jump. Ella sat down next to Meg and Johanna returned to her cushion, James sliding back over to his team. Charlotte pulled out gumballs from her pocket. "I brought them from home and don't worry my pocket is clean—"

"*Shhh!*" one of the boys said.

She popped a gumball in her mouth.

"Sit down!" a kid behind me said, but really, there was no place left for me and nobody made room. And honestly, I deserved it. So instead of wedging myself into the little spot between the cousins and Johanna, I decided to figure out about these sponsors.

Mallory and Alex sat in the back of the room by a display case lit in soft lights. I walked over to investigate, stepping over kids in flight suits from other Space Camp teams. Not all of them were doing robotics, but I tried figuring out which teams made up the remaining four teams competing on Thursday. Did anyone else have a sponsor yet?

My worries were momentarily pushed aside as my eyes fell on the display case filled with space rocks. Big and little meteorites that fell from the sky. Some of them were rough and pocked while others were smooth and shiny like pieces of marble.

"I thought you would like those," Mallory said. "You wrote about pallasites in your essay, but have you ever seen them in real life?"

I peered into the case. "No. Never," I breathed, because they were so weird and beautiful, like rocks with tiny stained glass windows everywhere.

She flipped a light on to illuminate the next display case, waving me closer. "What about an impactite?"

When a giant meteorite crashed into earth, the rocks on the ground could be liquefied upon impact. And that was exactly what the impactite in the display case looked like. Golden yellow, like honey. I couldn't believe it was ever a regular rock on the ground.

"It's from Arizona," Mallory said. "From a crater where a meteorite hit more than fifty thousand years ago."

And this was why I wanted to be an astronaut. Because everything about space and science was so cool. Liquefied rocks? Meteorites falling from space and making gigantic craters in the earth?

"All of these were collected by regular people. Anyone can be a scientist, you know." Mallory flicked the light back off, too bright in the darkened room.

I could have looked at space rocks for the rest of the night, but I had something else on my mind.

"So," I started, lowering my voice when the movie got quiet. "Some of the robotics teams are getting sponsors so they can buy cool parts for their rovers."

Mallory patted my shoulder. "I can't sponsor someone from my own team."

"But how do you find a sponsor?" My face burned because I should have read the orientation material and now it was obvious to everyone that I hadn't.

"Just ask someone," Mallory said, sitting back down in her chair. "Tell them about your project and if they like your idea, they might give you some bolts to get you started."

"Who should I ask?"

"Anyone who works here. The lady at the gift shop, the custodian in the dining hall, the chef. Find someone who's been here awhile, though. The longer they've worked at Space Camp, the more bolts they have to offer."

Alex leaned in. "But don't wait around. Sponsors go fast. However, earning the gyro sensor doesn't mean a sure win."

"But with the gyro sensor you can make your robot with only one or two wheels. Do you know how many parts you'd save like that? Gears and beams and not to mention a frame for—"

"We get it." Alex cut me off. "We're just saying, you can still win without a gyro sensor. The best scientists think with both sides of their brain. Getting creative is your specialty, right?"

I sighed, sitting in the chair next to Mallory. "That's my problem. I got a little too creative in the lab today and cost my team a bunch of bolts."

The movie screen showed a rocket blasting into space, making the entire room shake. Orion woke up. "BARK. BARK."

Mallory picked him up, petting his back like he was a real puppy. "Touch sensor," she said. "See? Three pats and he settles down." Orion got quiet again, closing his eyes and snoozing in her lap. "Anyway, do you think being too creative is the problem?"

I sighed. It was probably the fact that I ran with an idea without thinking it through. Or because I didn't talk to my team. Or maybe because I didn't read the orientation stuff. All of the normal things I did, or didn't do, if I was being honest.

"Just imagine if you were a team on the space station," Alex said. "You'd be in tight quarters, doing dangerous work, far from your family or friends. Without a good leader to get everyone working together, it could end in disaster."

I slouched in my seat. They were right. I was good at a lot of things, doing science experiments, knowing a lot about space rocks, math except for fractions. But maybe not so much at being a leader.

My heart panged. If I wasn't a good leader, would I ever be a good astronaut? Or a good big sister for that matter?

Mallory leaned over and deposited Orion into my lap. I patted his back three times and he lay back down. At least I was good at comforting a robotic dog.

"I do know of one guy who gives pretty hefty sponsorships," Mallory said.

"Really?" I brightened. Because that's all we needed to get back on track.

"Who?" Alex said. "Samuel?"

Mallory nodded. "But he's hard to find sometimes."

"Okay. Do you have any hints?" I asked.

"Just look for the guy with the robotic unicycle," Alex said.

"Robotic unicycle? But—"

"You'll have to figure out the rest on your own," Mallory said with a wink.

I sighed and sat on the ground with the other Space Campers and tried to focus on the movie. But I couldn't focus. How would I ever find the guy on the unicycle?

When the movie ended, Johanna and Charlotte ran up to me and I immediately noticed something.

"What happened to your names?" I pointed to the empty spaces on their flight suits where their glitter letters used to be.

Charlotte's face reddened. "Oh, it's no big deal." She patted me on the shoulder.

"Oh," I said. "Okay. Sure. Great."

Ella and Meg joined us and I couldn't even bear to look at them. Because it felt like a pretty big deal, actually.

Johanna bumped me with her hip. "It's okay, friend. They were falling off anyway."

But I knew they weren't.

"Mallory?" I said, after everyone started going to the stairs and back toward the habitat, Ella leading them of course. "Can I call my parents? I know it's late, but just to make sure they got home okay?"

Mallory looked at her watch. "You've got to make it quick." She waved me toward a phone booth.

As soon as my mom picked up the phone, I felt relieved.

"Luci?" she said, and then she called my dad over to share the line with her.

I wanted to tell them everything that had happened. With the robot. With mean Ella. But then I thought about all the astronauts on the Space Camp wall of fame. Did they call their parents on the first day of camp because they were homesick? I could pretty much guarantee they did not. "I'm just checking in. Making sure you guys are doing okay because I'm doing great over here," I lied.

"I'm so glad to hear that," Mom said. "I was worried you might feel a little homesick."

"I told you she'd be fine, dear," Dad said. "Didn't I say that?"

"Any news on Isadora?" I asked. Silence on the other end.

"Mom? Dad? What's going on?"

"Luci, we didn't want to worry you with this, but since you asked, I want to be honest," Mom said. "It seems that Isadora is no longer at the same orphanage."

"Where is she then?" I said, standing straighter.

"Transferred maybe or . . ."

My pulse started racing. "Or what?"

Mom's voice was softer now, the way it always got

when she had bad news like when my goldfish Sharky died or when Dad backed over my scooter with the car. "There's a small possibility there was a mix-up and maybe she went to another family."

I sucked in a breath.

"That's the worst-case scenario. Barely even possible, Luci," Dad added.

"How is that even a possibility at all?" I said. "You sent in the paperwork."

"I know," Mom said. "Abuelita is going to the orphanage tomorrow first thing in the morning. And the orphanage is looking into it; it's their top priority. We will figure this out and let you know as soon as we hear, okay?"

"This is nothing for you to worry about during your week of adventure," Dad said.

"But . . ." Did they not know how much I wanted Isadora to be my sister? Even though I would probably be a terrible sister anyway, never reading directions and always doing things without thinking. But, a baby sister . . . Isadora . . . I could learn to be better, couldn't I?

Mallory signaled to me. "All right," I said to my parents, knowing that it was almost time for lights-out. "But call me when you hear anything."

"We will," Mom promised.

"And no worrying allowed. We love you."

"Sure, Dad. I love you too."

And then they made kissing noises into the phone and we hung up.

CHAPTER 7

CAPSULE CREW

The RoboEngineers were late to the Mission Control Complex after breakfast the next day, so Mallory let us do a practice mission simulation to the International Space Station in the commercial crew vehicle. Charlotte and Meg followed Mallory to the mission control room and Johanna, Ella, and I stepped into the orbiter, clipping ourselves into our seats, putting the headphones on, and opening up the manuals in front of us.

"Capsule crew, do you copy?" I heard through my headset.

"We copy," Ella said. It was Charlotte on the other end, from down the hall in the mission control area.

"I copy too!" Meg piped in.

I turned to Johanna, sitting in the back of the orbiter, and she gave me a thumbs-up. I had had a lot of time to think about stuff overnight. There was nothing I could do to help look for Isadora while I was here at Space

Camp. What I *could* do was work on my big-sister skills. And that started with being a good team leader. So the first thing I had to do was find Samuel, the robotic unicycle guy, and he'd give us a big sponsorship and all of our problems would be solved. Mostly.

I twirled my purple hair, wishing that Raelyn could be here too. Anyway, she'd at least still be wearing her glitter name. She was used to my crazy ideas and she barely got mad at me when things went wrong. Except for the time we painted hearts on our foreheads with nail polish and then our moms wouldn't let us use nail polish remover on our skin to get them off. We had hearts on our heads for two days.

Mallory's voice came on over our headsets. "The right seat is the pilot." Ella smiled and I heard her sniff through the headphones. "The back seat is the mission specialist, and the commander is the front, left chair." Ella looked at me again, this time not smiling. It wasn't like I sat in this seat on purpose so I could be in charge again. If I was being honest, I was pretty sick of being in charge.

"Want to switch?" I asked.

Ella shook her head. "Whatever. I don't care."

But I knew she did.

"Launch ready in T-minus one minute and counting," Charlotte said from mission control.

"Really, Ella, if you want to switch," I said, putting a hand over my microphone.

She glared at me. "I'm fine, Luciana. Just don't let us crash or something."

"Well, I've never done this before, but I'm sure I can figure it out." I looked back at Johanna and she shrugged.

Ella let out a breath. "Let's just at least try to do *this* right, please?"

"What does that mean?" I felt a prick of anger in my chest because maybe I messed up on our first rover challenge and maybe I should have read the orientation materials a thousand times like some people, but I made a mistake which people do all the time and I was going to fix it.

"Guys," Charlotte said over the headset, "cut it out. Thirty seconds."

I looked at Ella. "I know a guy that might sponsor us."

"Nobody will sponsor a team with negative two million bolts!" Ella hit her forehead with her hand. "And we don't even have an idea for our competition robot yet."

"T-minus twenty seconds and *Ella stop it*," Charlotte said through the headset.

"No. I'm not going to stop it. The RoboEngineers paid one million bolts for an extra build session this morning in the lab. That's why they're late," Ella said. "They're going to be so far ahead of us!"

"Ten . . . nine . . . eight . . ." Charlotte said.

Johanna poked her head between us and patted us on our shoulders like robot puppies. "In Germany we are always talking about forgiveness." But Ella wasn't calming down.

"Six . . . five . . . four . . ."

"This would have never happened if I was in charge!" Ella yelled.

"And three-two-one-lift-off!" Charlotte said, extra loud in the headsets. "*You are lifting off into space. GET YOURSELVES TOGETHER.*"

And the screens in front of us that looked like windows to the outside showed our orbiter flashing through clouds and blue sky and then a burst of red from the rocket and we were in blackness, floating through space with the stars. I didn't know if it was the feeling of being in motion, or the fact that Ella was steaming mad at me over in the pilot seat, but I felt sick to my stomach.

We drifted in space for a few minutes in total silence except for someone chewing gum through the headset. And then we heard a *Beep! Beep! Beep!*

It was an anomaly. A problem.

I hit the big red button on my console. "Houston, we have a problem," I said like Mallory had instructed us.

"Hi, Luciana, all the way up in space!" It was Meg in mission control, and I couldn't help but smile a bit. "Okay, okay, locate F panel which is probably near the—"

"Got it," I said. "I mean, roger."

"Locate keypad."

I found the keypad on the F panel, lit up in red lights. "Roger."

"Ops, enter five . . . two . . . three . . . six . . . Oh, wait, I mean seven. Right. Okay, start over. Sorry!"

Johanna and I laughed, but Ella remained stone-faced. "Stop playing around, Meg."

"This is Mallory," we heard through the head-phones. "I'll reset the keypad." Had she been listening the entire time? "Okay, try it again."

"F panel, keypad. Here we go," Meg said. "Enter five . . . two . . . three . . . seven . . . nine . . . enter."

"Roger," I said.

"Good job," Meg said. "Anom—anomony resolved."

"Anom-oly," Ella corrected her.

We floated through space some more and Johanna had to prepare for docking with the ISS, all while I tried not to look at Ella. And I pretended like I hadn't heard her yell that she should have been in charge of the robotics team. Or that it felt like a punch to the gut or like getting a paper cut which also really hurt.

"Commander, prepare for docking to the ISS," Charlotte said and I sat up, straightening my headset and tightening my seat belt. I pressed a series of buttons and flipped a few switches, following the docking instructions in the checklist, wondering if this was what being the commander of a spacecraft really felt like.

"Pilot, begin docking," I said to Ella when we got into range. But she stayed frozen in her seat. Arms crossed. "Ella. Docking probe." We were closing in on the space station pretty quickly at this point. Johanna sat back in her chair, the image of the ISS flying at us through the capsule windows.

"Pilot," Charlotte said. "Pilot, please respond."

But it was no use. Ella wasn't going to respond.

I poked her arm, covering up my microphone with

my hand. "Come on, Ella. I said I was sorry like a trillion times." Frustration grew in my gut. I watched us hurtle toward the International Space Station. "We're roommates and on the same team, but you treat me like your enemy." And I remembered the unofficial camp law about roommates being friends, but did I even *want* to be friends with Ella when she was mean all the time?

I could see Johanna out of the corner of my eye about to say something, and I waved her off.

Ella looked at me, and for a second, her eyes softened. "I never said you were my enemy."

We plummeted through space and I stared at my commander's manual, helpless. And anyway, Ella didn't have to say I was her enemy for me to know it.

"We're going to crash!" Johanna shouted, covering her head with her arms.

"Pilot!" Charlotte urged from mission control. "Pilot! Engage docking probe!"

"Ella. You need to cooperate or you're going to fail the mission for everyone," Mallory warned.

With the threat of failure, Ella straightened her headset and got back on track, pushing buttons and pulling levers.

"Confirming that docking probe has been engaged," Charlotte said, out of breath. "You are free to dock."

I grabbed the joystick and steered us toward the target, but the joystick was hard to control and the spacecraft swerved and swung away from the ISS.

"Luci . . ." Johanna cautioned, and I tried harder to control the spacecraft.

I finally steadied the orbiter and lined up with the docking ring just in time to dock with the International Space Station. It wasn't perfect, but we also didn't crash in a ball of fire.

We heard cheers from mission control as we took our headsets off and left the capsule, successfully completing our mission.

Barely.

CHAPTER 8

JUNK PARTS

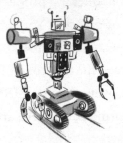

When we walked into the robotics lab after lunch, my stomach dropped. All of the robotics teams for the nine-to-eleven-year-old category were listed on the computer screen now, with their scores. The MarsBots, Wizards, and NinjaCoders each had three million bolts. The Space Heroes were in the lead with five million bolts, the RoboEngineers were close behind with four million, and we were in last place with negative two million.

I could feel James looking at me and I refused to turn away from the screen. Why did we have to share our lab time with the RoboEngineers? Why not the Wizards or some other team that didn't include James?

Johanna read the challenge for the day off the board. ". . . for three million bolts, fix the broken robot . . ." There were seven robots, standing still and slack on the tile floor. Some had claws, others had pinchers, and one had a hammer. "I got this," Johanna said, running to pick a robot.

"How about we split up? Half of us start on the competition robot and the other half do the challenge with Johanna?" I said.

Meg raised her hand. "I pick Johanna!" And she raced off.

Charlotte and Ella stayed with me although Ella stood frozen, looking at the scoreboard still, her arms crossed. Charlotte nudged her but she wouldn't move. So Charlotte reached out and pinched her.

"Ow, Charlotte!" Ella squealed. "Why are you always doing that?"

Charlotte shook her head. "Can we just start working together, please? Luci's right, we're on the same team, Ella. You're ruining everything like you always do."

Ella uncrossed her arms, looking hurt. "I never ruin everything!"

"It's like if you're not in charge then forget about anyone else having any fun or doing anything at all and if we were at home right now, you'd quit and spend the rest of the time sulking and this is why you don't have any friends anymore." Charlotte took a giant breath.

"Come on, guys," I said, not sure if I should stay out of it. "Don't fight."

"WE'RE NOT FIGHTING," they both yelled at the same time.

"No one is ruining anything," I said. "Except for maybe me, but we've already gone over how I'm going to fix it."

Ella snorted and Charlotte sent her a warning glare.

"Mallory told me about a guy who gives out big sponsorships, and I know you don't think we can get a sponsor with our terrible score right now, but there's no reason why we shouldn't try." James and the rest of the RoboEngineers were hunched over a logbook with rulers and calculators like they were making secret robot plans.

"Where is this guy?" Charlotte asked.

"Well," I said, making a face. "He's not easy to find apparently. But he rides a robotic unicycle, so how hard could it be, really?"

Actually, maybe really hard, because Space Camp was big and, according to Mallory and Alex, sponsors went fast.

Ella blew air out of her mouth. "Fine, we'll look for your robot-unicycle guy later. But can we design our competition robot *now*?"

Charlotte clapped and hugged her. "See? There you go, Ella! Now we're working together. That wasn't so hard."

Ella punched her in the shoulder.

James and his team were hanging out mysteriously in the closet by the parts wall. So that's where Ella, Charlotte, and I started.

"What are you guys doing?" I asked, peeking into the closet. Plastic tubs for each team sat on metal shelves that lined the walls. The RoboEngineers had their own tub on the floor with what appeared to be the start of a robot inside. Mallory, Leo, and Alex sat nearby around a trash can, sorting through a container of old parts.

"No cheating!" James squawked, trying to get in front of his robot.

Ella stepped up. "We don't cheat."

"Yeah," Charlotte said. "We win."

And I felt a rush of pride and happiness because it felt good to all be on the same side.

The RoboEngineers slid their tub out of the closet, glaring at us.

Mallory tossed a broken tread into the trash can with a thump.

"Hey," I said. "Can we have a look?"

Mallory waved me over. "Sure. It's mostly junk, but feel free." She picked up a cracked rubber gasket and flung it into the trash can.

Charlotte, Ella, and I looked into the boxes of parts on the floor. Lots of old batteries and ancient broken motors, a few chargers with obvious damage, and one entire bin of robot legs.

"What's this?" I said, pulling a part from under a pile of gears.

Leo held out a hand for a closer look. "Ah, I remember when we had these," he said. "It's an old motor module for a walking robot."

"A walking robot? You don't use these anymore?"

He shrugged his shoulders. "Everyone wants to build a rolling rover these days."

I thought of all the books I'd been reading on Mars rovers and how the rocky terrain was causing damage to their wheels.

I turned to Charlotte and Ella, both doubled over, leaning into a bin of building bricks and beams. "What if we made a walking rover?" I held out the part. "It's a motor module. You plug in a bunch of legs."

Ella looked skeptical.

"It would probably climb right up that rocky slope to the space elevator no problem and it would be different than everyone else's rover." Which was the wrong thing to say to follow-the-rules Ella. "I mean, not different, but unique in a scientific way." I set the part down and pulled out my Space Camp logbook and pencil from one of the many pockets of my flight suit. I sketched my idea and held up my drawing. "Like this."

Ella was still unconvinced, looking around the closet. "We're already so behind. We should just try to make the simplest robot we can and earn some points back."

"Hey," I said to the crew trainers. "How many bolts would an old part like this cost?"

Leo looked up and thought for a moment. "Free, I guess. If you pulled it from these junk bins, and it works, it's all yours, no charge."

Ella lit up. "Like, all of these parts are free?"

"Yes." Leo tossed a broken wheel set into the trash can. "Just know that most of them are broken so it might not be worth the time you'll lose on troubleshooting."

Charlotte stepped out of the closet and pulled some bricks and wheels from the parts containers outside. "This right here would cost us more than a million bolts," she said to us.

I nudged Ella with my shoulder. "You want to make a junkyard robot?"

Johanna and Meg rushed into the closet, holding up the challenge robot. "Done! That's an extra three million bolts for team Red Rovers!"

Ella grabbed the robot, looking it up and down. "You guys fixed this?" She looked at the clock on the wall. "That fast?"

Meg bounced on her feet. "I pretty much watched. Johanna did it all. She's like a robot-fixing genius."

Johanna swung her arms back and forth, embarrassed. "I like to take things apart and put them back together."

I glanced out at the scoreboard. We were still behind all of the teams by at least five million bolts, and it would be even more once the rest of the teams fixed their own robots. I looked at the motor module. Free parts were probably our only chance at catching up.

Johanna set down her robot and showed the group how she'd got it working again.

"Amazing," Charlotte said.

I grabbed a screwdriver from the shelf behind me and unscrewed the battery door on the motor module, pulling out the old batteries. "Oh no," I whispered, because battery acid had flooded the battery compartment. I tapped Johanna on the shoulder. "You think you can fix this?"

"Hmmm," she said, taking the part from me, "this happens to my brother's toys all the time." And then she disappeared back into the robotics lab, the rest of us following her.

The RoboEngineers were hard at work at one of the tables, and as we passed, they dove over their creation so we couldn't see anything.

"Puh-lease," Meg said, rolling her eyes.

We had barely sat down at our own table, the farthest one from the RoboEngineers, when Johanna was back, skipping across the lab. "Try it." She handed me the batteries and I popped them in. A green light glowed from the battery pack.

I grinned.

"Here, put these in," Charlotte said, leaning over the table and depositing six beams in front of me. Robot legs. I popped them into the motor module and turned it on. The robot's legs went crazy, waving in the air, moving in synch.

I put the rover on the table and it skittered across the surface, Johanna grabbing it before it fell off.

"It works!" I said. "This is amazing! We could make our rover out of all the junk parts and it wouldn't cost us anything."

Johanna inspected the motor module. "Yes, I love that idea."

"We are going to have the best rover!" Meg said. "The best, best, best one!"

James walked by, eyeing my logbook open to the sketch of our walking robot.

"Nice art project."

I flipped it closed and we all lunged for the parts scattered on the table at once, Johanna passing the motor module to Meg, telling her to put it back in our box where it would be safest. We hid the rest of the parts in our pockets and stuffed them under our arms until James finally wandered away.

We looked at Ella, standing over the robot legs with her arms crossed.

"What do you think, cousin?" Charlotte said.

Ella looked up, and maybe she even had a small smile on her face. "I'm in."

And together, as a team, the Red Rovers raided the broken parts closet.

CHAPTER 9

MISSING MODULE

The next day Mallory walked us through the Space Camp gift shop on our way back from doing the MAT, otherwise known as the Multi-Axis Trainer. It was part of the astronaut training program in the 1960s and had been used to simulate a spacecraft that was spinning out of control in space. At least, that's what our logbook said. And I knew this because I was the kind of person who read logbooks now.

Meg shuffled behind us all, mad at herself because she had been too scared to try it. Even after Mallory had told her nobody in all of her five years of working there had ever thrown up or fallen over from dizziness. Not to mention the boys had been pretty hard on her for not being brave, which had started a James versus Ella fight all over again. Big sisters didn't let anyone mess with their little sisters. I was taking all sorts of notes from Ella. I knew I shouldn't worry so much about Isadora, but I couldn't help myself. The orphanage would find her, right?

"Five minutes," Mallory said, waving her hands across the giant store. "And then we have to get to the lab. Make your wish list and come back later to buy."

We scattered, Charlotte and Johanna going for the rack of sweatshirts, Meg for the bin of spiky balls. Ella and I looked at the astronaut suits.

"Can you imagine?" I said. "These would be so awesome for Halloween."

She nodded her head.

I saw a giant rack of postcards. One said "Somebunny had fun at Space Camp!" with a bunny wearing a flight suit and chewing on hydroponic greens. It had Raelyn's name written all over it. Ella just stood there, looking at her fingernails. "Look, Ella, for my best friend back home." I held up the postcard, trying to be extra friendly. "She has a real bunny. It's so perfect!"

Ella gave me a little smile. "Sure."

And then I remembered what Meg had said about Ella having no friends. I looked around the store, trying to change the subject. "Are you going to get anything?"

She was still looking at the postcard. "My best friend

doesn't have a bunny, and actually, we're not even best friends anymore."

"Why not?"

She sniffed and shuffled her feet. "It's what happens when someone moves away. They just stop texting and returning your phone calls because of all their new best friends. But it's fine."

"How long were you best friends?"

"Since kindergarten," she said.

Six years. The same as Raelyn and me.

"She moved a few months ago," Ella said, pulling out a postcard that said "Actually I *am* a Rocket Scientist!" with a picture of the *Saturn V* under a Space Camp logo.

"I bet she misses you a lot."

"If she missed me, she'd call me and ask how school is going. Also, we had this thing where we'd think up really bad jokes and she doesn't even do that anymore."

"Maybe she doesn't have a thousand new best friends and she's feeling really homesick."

Ella put the postcard back.

"Maybe she needs you more than ever," I said, looking at my bunny postcard.

Mallory was waving from the front door. Time to go.

"Or maybe not," Ella said, shrugging. And then she walked away before I could tell her the story about Raelyn and me and how in third grade we almost stopped being best friends.

When we got to the robotics lab, everyone was already there and staring at the scoreboard. The MarsBots had caught up to the Space Heroes over-night, putting James's team in third place with seven million bolts.

"The MarsBots must have found a sponsor," Johanna said.

The top two teams were only two million bolts away from claiming the gyro sensor. It was a race to get the most bolts, and from the look of it, the RoboEngineers were not happy.

As for our team, we were still way behind. Not to mention I still hadn't seen any signs of a guy on a robot unicycle or been able to find us any other sponsors. There weren't many left at this point. All the museum tour guides were out of bolts. So were the scuba divers who taught lessons in the astronaut training pool. And when I asked the chef in the crew galley, all she had to offer was a bowl of fried pickles.

I pulled out my logbook, flipping to the page with our robot ideas.

"Are you making a walking robot?" James said.

"Yep!" Meg said before we could grab her.

"Can't share that information with you," I said, flapping my logbook closed. "Top secret."

"Where did you find the parts for that?" he asked.

"None of your business," Ella said, pushing in between us. "Snoop."

"Be nice, Ella," Charlotte said.

"Forget it," he said.

Charlotte rushed over to the challenge board and clapped next to us. "It's a programming challenge, my very favorite kind of robotics challenge and can I do it, please, guys?"

The rest of our team looked at one another and laughed. Charlotte plopped herself in front of a series of computer screens. "Meg," she said. "Sit." She patted the seat next to her.

Meg skipped over, and the rest of us got started sifting through the junk parts in the closet, looking for any sensors that seemed remotely workable.

"If Charlotte and Meg do today's challenge, we'll

get another three million bolts," Johanna said. "We'll even be ahead of the Wizards." Apparently they had bought a special color sensor from the parts wall, bringing their bolts down to three million.

"If the RoboEngineers cash in their bolts for the gyro sensor," I said, "we'll be ahead of them too."

"Not for long," Ella said. "Their robots will be faster and better in the competition. We won't even be able to compete."

I pulled out a sensor that had no obvious damage, but Johanna shook her head. "Toss."

I threw it in the trash.

We were deep into our search for parts when bells and whistles and an audio of clapping and cheering went off, bringing everyone to a screeching halt. Johanna and I looked out to the lab and saw Leo hand James the gyro sensor. They had already completed the programming challenge and made it to ten million bolts. We watched the scoreboard, and team RoboEngineers went all the way back down to zero, which was partially satisfying, except we knew they were probably going to win the competition anyway.

The lab got quiet after that, the RoboEngineers

moving to a secret location to continue working on their robot, and soon it was only us with the entire robotics lab to ourselves.

We took our plastic tub full of parts back to a table to get started on building.

"Hey, Luci." Ella sifted through the bin. "Where's the motor module?"

"It's in there," I said, handing Johanna a busted-up claw attachment.

"Nope," Ella said. "It's not in here." She dumped out the parts and shuffled through them.

I stood next to her. "I thought Meg put it back in our tub. Meg?" I called. "Did you put the motor module back?"

Meg barely looked up from programming with Charlotte. "Yep! Back in the box like Johanna said."

"But it's not here," Ella said, and she was right, it wasn't.

We checked the parts closet, inspecting the floor and the dark corners, sifting through the trash cans of broken parts. Getting desperate, I grabbed my Space Camp backpack from a hook on the wall, zipped open the outer pockets, and reached around inside. Yesterday, when we had been trying to hide our parts from the

RoboEngineers, we had stuffed parts everywhere. But there was nothing there.

I squatted on the floor, opening the drawstring top and searching inside. Colored pencils. A Space Camp hoodie. A map of the grounds and sunblock. No walking motor module. My heart started beating faster and I overturned my bag, dumping everything on the floor. My colored pencils rolled everywhere.

"Luciana?" Mallory said, coming over. And basically none of the Red Rovers were working anymore, kind of frozen in place because they all knew what was happening. The part was gone.

I shuffled through all of my papers again, but it was no use. The part was officially missing. "Meg? Are you sure-sure-sure you put the part back?"

"Yes!" she said.

"Check your flight suits," Johanna said. "All of your pockets."

We patted our suits, checking all the little zipped pockets and buttoned up hidey-holes. Nothing.

"We lost it?" Ella said.

No. I shook my head. No way we could have lost something like this.

"It's gone?" Charlotte joined us, stepping away from the computer program, Meg linked to her elbow.

"Or maybe it got stolen." I said it out loud and in my head at the exact same time and it all fell into place. James asking us all these questions. The RoboEngineers building their robot in a secret location. They stole our part to use it themselves.

The girls unfroze and I saw in their faces that they knew it too. We had been sabatoged.

"Wait a minute," Mallory said. "You're jumping to conclusions. Messing with another team's project is a big deal that we don't take lightly here."

My mind was whirling. Would James want to win so badly that he'd risk everything?

"But we're not even a threat to their team," Ella said, apparently also thinking that James's team was the culprit.

"Maybe we had the part they want," I said. "Maybe they want to make a walking robot too."

"Actually," Johanna said, "a gyro sensor would go perfectly with a walking robot. He could make it a biped and then use the rest of the legs to hold tools." She nodded. "Brilliant."

Ella sighed. "I hate to say it, but maybe you're right. All he talks about is winning."

"These are some serious accusations," Mallory said, unhooking Orion from a charging station on the wall. "I want you guys to think this over before you assume the part was stolen. Okay? Look everywhere."

Orion zoomed toward Leo in the parts closet, Mallory following him.

I heard what Mallory said, but we had already looked everywhere. The only logical answer was that James and his team had stolen the part. "We can't let him get away with this," I said to the group as soon as she was out of earshot.

"What are we supposed to do now?" Ella said. "Without the motor module, we'd have to start our robot from scratch! There's no time for that! I mean, have you even seen any wheel sets we could salvage from the junk closet?"

We shook our heads. Most of the broken wheels and treads were beyond repair.

"So then, where would we get the bolts to buy all the parts we'd need?" We looked at the screen. We had one million bolts, and completing the programming challenge for the day would only bring us to four million.

My mind spiraled. I should have hid the motor module, and not let Meg put it in our bin, in plain sight.

"Seriously, guys," Charlotte said. "What are we going to do?"

Really, there was only one thing to do. That motor module was ours, and as the captain, I couldn't let my team lose because of a cheater like James. And since Mallory didn't believe us, we'd have to fix this on our own.

"I know exactly what we're going to do," I said. Everyone stopped and looked at me. "We're going to get that part back."

CHAPTER 10

THE PLAN

The rest of the day, we worked on our Motor Module Take-Back Plan.

"Should we do it during the Mars viewing?" Charlotte asked.

We were performing soil experiments, looking for different soil components, in the greenhouse, surrounded by leafy green hydroponics. Afterward we were going to have a picnic dinner under the *Pathfinder*. Mars was in the perfect position for viewing tonight.

"We can't all go missing at the same time though. That would look totally obvious and suspicious," she continued.

"Hand me the soil sample," Meg said, her safety goggles too big on her face.

Johanna handed her a tube of soil marked "Regolith A." "I'll stay at the Mars viewing if you want me to," Meg offered.

"Maybe just you and Ella should go," Charlotte told me, holding a beaker full of water in her hand.

I looked at Ella and she actually smiled at me. "Yeah, okay."

"You can't leave me," Meg said. "Not outside in the pitch-black dark."

"Charlotte and Johanna will be there," I said, but Ella and Charlotte both shook their heads.

"You don't know what it's like to have a little sister," Ella said, but then her ears turned red. "I mean . . . not because you—"

"I know you didn't mean it like that," I said, but if I was being honest, she was right. I didn't know the first thing about being a big sister. And then I started worrying about Isadora all over again. "You can come with us, Meg," I said, pushing the bad thoughts from my head.

Meg looked at the ground. "I know I'm kind of old to be scared of so many things; it's just, I can't help it."

Charlotte and Ella squeezed Meg into a hug. "We love you. Scaredy-pants or not."

"Hey!" Meg said, swatting at Ella, but then they were both laughing and falling over on each other and I felt a pang in my belly. A left-out kind of feeling, a missing-home-worried kind of feeling.

Johanna dumped the "Regolith B" sample into a beaker and added a few drops of ethanol, swirling it around to mix. "I think that's too many people, though. If you all leave for so long, Mallory might go look for you."

"What if we waited until after lights-out?" I suggested.

Everyone went quiet, clearly not a fan of my idea.

Ella looked up from her sample. "That would be totally breaking the rules. And we would already be breaking the rules by wandering around alone, without our trainer."

Charlotte shook her head. "What about the night-time crew trainers that will be everywhere and also the security guards? We'll get kicked out—"

"Charlotte's right," Johanna said. "All of this sounds too risky."

"Then let me do it alone," I said.

Charlotte held out a tube for Ella and she scooped in some of the soil sample.

"No way," Ella said. "We do it together. We're a team."

Charlotte smiled at Ella. "Wow, listen to you, team player."

Ella rolled her eyes.

"We'll get caught for sure," Meg whined.

Johanna looked up from the sample beaker. "Actually, we could go the back way to the lab. It's kind of secret."

"There's a back way?" I said.

She finished pouring water into a graduated cylinder and then snapped her gloves off. "Through that hall across from the Space Camp store in the common area."

"The hall of artifacts?" Ella said.

Meg whimpered, and in all honesty, this new information did not thrill me either.

"Yes, that's the one. It leads to the hallway behind the galley and robotics lab. There's a back entrance. Alex took me that way once when I needed a pair of pliers."

"Time's up," Mallory said, poking her head into the greenhouse. "Clean up and we'll head to the galley and then outside for the Mars viewing."

We were quiet as we cleaned up our soil experiment, all of us probably thinking about sneaking out that night. It was risky for sure and even I knew it was against the rules big time. But, as their captain, was I supposed to just let James steal from us like that? It was my job to get us those "Best Rover" patches at the end of the week, so really, what choice did we have?

We barely ate anything off our trays that night and while the boys wanted a thousand looks through the telescope, we only took one each.

"Come on, girls," Mallory said, tugging on Meg's ponytail. "Are you all getting sick on me?"

It sure felt like that actually, my stomach churning and my heart beating too fast. We looked at one another.

"Just tired," Ella said.

"Yep," Meg said. "I've never been so tired in my whole life." She yawned dramatically and stretched her arms out wide.

The Mars viewing took forever and when it was finally lights-out, we said good night to Alex and Mallory and Orion and watched them close the doors to their own rooms next to ours.

"Don't fall asleep," I whispered in the quiet room.

Meg flicked on one of her flashlights. "I'm getting sleepy," she said. "How long do we have to stay up?"

Ella peered down into my bunk. "What's the plan?"

I rolled out of bed, tiptoeing to the door to peek through the peephole. Light was still coming from Mallory's room, illuminating the dark hallway.

"We have to wait until Mallory goes to sleep," I said, and Johanna was beside me, nudging me over to see for herself, her hair pulled into a messy ponytail, wearing a rainbow unicorn robe.

"That could take a long, long time. I just want to get this done with."

I patted Johanna on the shoulder. "It will be fine. We can do this."

She nodded her head, shuffling back to her bed. "Yes." She yawned. "We can do this."

I grabbed her and redirected her to the carpet. "You've got to stay awake, Johanna. It won't be long."

Ella took her turn looking out the peephole. "Come on, Mallory, lights-out," she whispered as if Mallory would be able to hear her.

Charlotte padded over to us on the rug, hooking a thumb in Ella's direction. "I'm proud of her. I never would have believed she'd be sneaking out of the bunk at night to steal back a rover part."

Ella turned away from the door, whispering, "It's all about justice, you know? Luci is right."

That was nearly three times now that Ella was nice to me. Almost friendly, even. Maybe it was from all my friend advice in the gift shop or the fact that we were taking down her nemesis together. I was fine with either of those scenarios if it meant we could all start being friends.

"Mallory won't do anything about it, without proof, and James will never admit he's cheating. So it's up to us to set it right." Ella looked back through the peephole. "Um. Guys? Mallory's light is out." She looked pale even in the glow-stick-lit room.

I swallowed hard, my heart thumping all the way up to my throat.

"If we get caught, do you think they'll call our parents?" Meg said. "What if they send us home?"

I stood up. "We don't have to do this, guys. It's okay. I can go by myself."

We stood in a circle. All of us were strangers a few days ago, and now we were a team. Friends. Unlikely friends, some of us, which made it feel that much cooler. Whatever they decided would be okay with me. I couldn't ask my team to take such a risk. Not as their captain.

"We're all going," Ella said.

And so it was decided.

"Are your pajamas glowing in the dark?" Charlotte said to Meg as soon as I put my hand on the doorknob. "We can't have us glowing down the hall like that and also we'll get caught for sure."

"Oh." She flicked off her flashlight. Her shirt lit up with green stars in the darkness, constellations drawn together in bright white. "Yep."

"We need to do something about that," Ella said.

"Here." Johanna pulled off her robe and handed it to Meg.

"I love-love-love unicorns and rainbows!" Meg said.

I inched the door open. "*Shhh!*"

The hallway was empty, so I signaled for everyone to move forward with me. Halfway out of the room, we heard a door slam. I turned around, waving frantically for everyone to push back into our room, except we were so clumped up, we got stuck in the doorframe and I was still in the complete open hallway when Noah shuffled past.

"Hey," he said, stopping and squinting at me. He wasn't wearing his glasses. "Luci?"

"Um, hey," I said. "Just getting a drink of water."

He lingered for a moment longer before starting back down the hall again. And with one more look over his shoulder in my direction, he disappeared into the bathroom.

LIGHTS-OUT
BREAK-OUT

We squeezed back into our room and I watched through the peephole until Noah walked past again. When we heard the click of his habitat door, we started over, sneaking out of our room. As soon as we slipped into the hall outside, I immediately regretted that everyone had come along. With all the breathing and swishing of clothes and tip-tapping of slippers, five people walking stealthily together sounded far louder than I had imagined. I kept waving my hand to tell everyone to keep it down, until we were barely inching our way along.

Ella and I took the lead, Meg hanging off Ella's elbow because we wouldn't let her turn on her flashlight. And even though Johanna's robe covered up the bright glowing of Meg's shirt, it didn't reach all the way down to the constellations on her pajama bottoms. If we ran into anyone on our mission, we'd be easily spotted.

"Watch the stairs," I warned, slowing the group down, taking each step carefully. If one person missed a step and stumbled, it would be a five-kid pileup at the bottom. And it would be really hard to explain to Mallory why we were all piled at the bottom of the stairs in the middle of the night.

I breathed a sigh of relief when we all safely got to the bottom. We had to go the long way around the common area, staying in the shadows, because the galley's lights were still on above the drink station and we knew the nighttime crew trainer was around somewhere. We paused for a minute by the wall of Space Camp graduates.

"Did you hear something?" Ella asked.

We held our breaths listening, but no, there were no sounds anywhere. Space Camp was sleeping, all except for the five girls from Habitat 4b.

I motioned us toward the displays of meteorites and space rocks, past the pillows and beanbags against the wall for after-dinner movies, and stopped in the gaping dark entrance to the hall of artifacts.

Meg buried her face in Ella's chest.

"There are no stuffed monkeys. They are not real," Ella said.

"We can't just stand here, Meg," I said, glancing over my shoulder.

"It's not her fault," Ella said, glaring at me. "She's scared."

Johanna stepped up. "Meg," she said, leaning over. "You are so brave. Look at you. You've gotten this far without a flashlight or anything! Come on, let's make socks."

Meg looked at her. "Let's make . . . what?"

"Socks," Johanna repeated. "Like, let's go! We can do this! It's what we say in Germany."

And with that, Meg straightened up. "Okay, then, let's make socks!" She grabbed Ella's hand and led us into the dark hallway. My face burned. Johanna knew how to talk to a little sister. I had so much to learn.

Empty astronaut suits loomed over us in display cases. Face masks hung from the walls and we stepped around a roped-off exhibit of old space equipment. Suddenly, a light went on, flooding the common area. We froze, pushing glow-in-the-dark Meg into the middle of our circle, bending and squeezing into a little group. I watched the common area with one peeking eye and sucked in a breath, because someone was zipping around the crew galley.

I tapped everyone on the shoulder, fast and furious, because the guy, now standing still in front of the coffee machine, had a robotic unicycle, glowing in purple and blue neon lights. If we weren't huddled together in criminal secrecy, I would have jumped up and down like a maniac.

Everyone's eyes got big and we shuffled as a group farther into the shadows of the artifacts, watching the mystery guy zip back out of the galley and down the hallway in the opposite direction. Johanna tugged on my sleeve when he stopped at a door at the far end.

"What's that say on his door?" she said.

I squinted, but the sign was too far away, and he opened the door and disappeared inside.

"Who drinks coffee at this hour?" Charlotte asked.

We shushed her and took careful steps down the rest of the hall until we turned the corner, safe from being seen by a random glance in our direction.

We fast-walked the rest of the way through the artifacts. "I think this is the door," Johanna said in a whisper. "Give me your flashlight, Meg."

I looked at my watch, getting nervous. We'd been breaking the rules for nearly twenty minutes at this point and still didn't have the motor module. Not to mention there were quite a few doors in this hallway, and how were we going to find the one that led to the back of the robot lab without taking forever?

"Nope," Johanna said. "Next one."

It wasn't that one either, but at the next one Johanna finally stopped. "I have a feeling this is the one. Here. I can see the wall of plastic bricks."

I looked up at the ceiling and even though there were no twinkling stars, I wished that the door was unlocked. *Please, please, let the door be unlocked.*

Click.

"It's open," Ella whispered.

We pushed into the robotics lab, shutting the door behind us and piling in. We stepped over boxes and half-built towers of connectors and a giant beach ball made entirely of beams and struts. The building area of the lab was tinged in red from the blipping of the computer monitors. Our scores were displayed on the screen on the wall and we were still in last place. But not for long, I hoped.

We entered the supply closet and searched for the RoboEngineers' plastic tub. Most of the tubs had rovers inside of them at this point in the week, with the final competition so close. One of the teams had a rover so tall, the lid to their tub didn't even fit.

"Found it," Johanna said. She slid the tub from the shelf and put it on the floor, the rest of us kneeling beside it.

Their tub was full of robot parts, claws, and wheels, and even a hammer made out of bricks. "Cool," Johanna said, pulling out a scooper attachment. "Someone made this."

"Wow, they're pretty good at building," Charlotte said.

So far there was no sign of our motor module. Johanna put down the flashlight and she and I carefully lifted their robot out of the tub and laid it on the floor to better see the rest of the parts in their tub.

"Someone grab our tub off the shelf, please?" I said.

Ella and Meg both stood up.

"Watch out," Charlotte said and I heard something hit the floor, the beam of light flicking off.

"Was that the flashlight?" I said. "Someone pick it up. I can't see any—"

And then there was a different sound. A clattering and splintering sound beside me.

"No." It was Ella. "No-no-no-no . . ."

"What was that?" Charlotte asked.

I groped the floor for the flashlight until I found it at someone's slippered foot. When I turned it on, we found Ella standing over what was left of James's team's rover.

"I . . ." She covered her face. "I lost my balance . . . I didn't mean . . ."

"Ohno, ohno, ohno, ohno . . ." Charlotte said and the rest of us froze. What had we done?

Ella dropped to the floor, her head in her hands.

Meg stood there, holding tub number eight. She popped the lid off the plastic bin. "Uh, guys? Isn't this the motor module?"

Everyone looked up and I scrambled off the floor to see what she was holding. It was definitely our motor module and I grabbed it, all of us crowding around, checking for damage with the flashlight, in case the RoboEngineers had tampered with it. But it was okay. Someone had simply just put it in another box.

"What?" Johanna shook her head. "He put it in another tub? To trick us? *Wie gemein!*"

"Did you just say a bad word?" Charlotte asked.

Johanna blew out a breath. "No, it means, like, how mean that he could do that."

It dawned on me. The perfect plan. James and his team had stolen our part and then hidden it in another plastic tub so no one would ever know they'd done it.

"No," Meg said. "Johanna told me to put the part away. She said to go put the part in our box. So I put it in number eight."

I smacked my head. "No, Meg. We're box *eighteen*."

Ella stood up. "Meg! Why didn't you say something before?"

Meg's face turned so red, I could see it even in the dim light. "I . . . I . . . you said it was stolen. I thought it was stolen!"

"Why didn't you check the box when everyone else was looking?" I said. "If you knew you had put it in box eight, why didn't you look there?"

Meg was crying now.

"All you had to do was look, Meg—"

Ella grabbed the flashlight from me, shining it in my face. "Leave her alone, Luciana. Stop."

"I thought . . . It was an accident . . . I thought someone else had already looked there . . ."

I felt a crushing feeling in my body because Ella was right. This wasn't Meg's fault, it was mine. I was the one who had jumped to the conclusion that the part was stolen. I was the one who wanted to prove that I had what it took to be a good leader. "Meg," I said. "I'm sorry, Meg, it's not your fault." I tried to hug her, but she squeezed in closer to Ella. I was going to be the worst big sister in the entire history of the planet. The worst. Actually, what was I even good at anymore? Forget about showing everyone that I had what it took to be an astronaut. Forget about everything.

"This whole time, James was innocent," Charlotte said, and I could feel her looking at me through the darkness.

Just another situation when I'd acted too fast. When I didn't think. Ella shined the flashlight on the broken robot.

"Can you fix it, Johanna?" she asked through the quiet.

Johanna's head shook in the shadows. "*Nein.* It's going to cost them a lot of bolts."

"We can give them all of ours!" Meg said, popping up.

Charlotte sighed. "With all of our bolts together, they'd barely be able to replace two of their sensors, not to mention the competition is the day after tomorrow and how are they going to rebuild that fast?"

Johanna knelt on the floor, placing robot parts back in their plastic tub. She held up one of the sensors. "See? *Kaputt.* Cracked."

Ella sniffed, and together with Meg, she joined Johanna.

"What's going to happen?" Meg said, whispering, her throat sounding swollen from crying.

"I can't get sent home," Johanna said. "My family saved for this camp for so long . . ." She wiped her face and Charlotte reached over and hugged her.

Meg and Ella joined the hug. Then it was just me, standing there by myself next to a lump of robot parts, the cold of the cement floor seeping through my slippers.

CHAPTER 12

EMERGENCY MEETING

I couldn't sleep that night. Not even when we were all safely back in our habitat. Not even when I heard the sleeping sounds of the rest of my bunkmates. I couldn't stop thinking about how maybe I'd just ruined my chances at ever becoming an astronaut. Because if I couldn't make it through Space Camp, how could I ever make it through real astronaut training?

The sun was barely up when I finally gave in, slid out of bed, and padded down the stairs to the common area. Unlike last night, the area was lit up and the galley was a flurry of activity. Cooks flipping pancakes, frying up everyone's favorite star-shaped tator tots. Getting ready to start another day at Space Camp. Thanks to me, though, there was a chance it would be Habitat 4b's last one.

The rocket phone booths were empty, so I closed

myself into the first one and dialed my parents' number. If anyone knew what to do, it would be them.

"Luci?" Mom picked up on the first ring.

"Hi Mom," I said.

"You're calling so early. Is everything okay?" Her voice didn't sound like her normal voice, almost like the phone was too far from her face.

"Mom?"

"Sweetie, we're on the line with Abuelita . . ." And then I heard her talking to Dad, muffled, almost like she had her hand over the phone speaker.

"Mom? What—"

"Abuelita is trying to help us because . . ." She took a deep breath into the phone, and then she was gone again, speaking to Dad in a low voice.

"What? Is it Isadora?" My heart was racing again. Not the baby. Please. Please. Not the baby.

Dad got on the line, clearing his throat, and I could hear Mom blowing her nose in the background.

"Luci, they've located Izzy."

"That's good, right?" My entire body was thumping, my pulse in my ears. I cracked the phone booth door, cool air trickling in. "Right?"

"She's in the hospital, Luciana," Dad said.

"Oh, no. Why?" I got frustrated; my parents were taking too long to answer my questions. "Dad, is she okay?"

"Abuelita is on her way to the hospital now, but it seems that she is very sick. We do not know many details."

And then we were both silent for a minute because what was there to say? How could nobody know anything more? How was it that we weren't running to the airport right now to be with her?

"Luci?"

I shut the door to the phone booth again and leaned against the glass. "I want to be with her. I want to go to Chile."

Dad took a breath. "I know, honey, I know. This is hard, but we are so lucky to have Abuelita close by. We just found this out a few minutes ago and there are a lot of questions we still need answered, Luci." He paused. "For all we know this could be a mistake and Abuelita will get there to find the baby is not Isadora at all. We will wait and be patient."

I stood up again, wiping my face. The common area was starting to fill with campers.

"Sweetheart," Dad said. "We did not want to burden you with this information until we knew more. I am so sorry."

I didn't know what to say except that it felt like everything was falling apart at the same time.

"Is everything okay at camp?" he said. "Are you okay? Happy?"

"I—" But then I couldn't tell him. Not with the news about Izzy. "I was just calling to check in."

"Hey, Luci?" Dad said, talking fast all of a sudden. "That's Abuelita calling us back. Let me take that. I'll call you when we hear something. Okay? Love you!"

And then he hung up.

I stumbled out of the phone booth and for a minute all I could do was stand there, watching campers lining up for breakfast, buying gum and ChapStick and pens at the Space Camp store, digging through the lost-and-found bin.

And then someone called my name.

"Luci!" It was Johanna, waving from the top of the stairs. She ran down to the common area. "Mallory is looking for you. We didn't know where you went. We haven't told her anything, by the way." She looked at my face. "Are you okay?"

I flopped onto one of the giant pillows on the floor. "They found Izzy. My little sister. She is in the hospital."

Johanna sat next to me. "She's sick?"

"They're not even sure it's her, but if it is, yes, my dad said she is very sick."

Johanna sucked in a breath. "No. *Das tut mir Leid.*"

I looked at her and she said, "I am so sorry for you."

"Well, maybe all of this is happening because I would be a terrible big sister," I said. "Maybe someone figured out that I'm a really bad role model."

Johanna shook her head. "No, no, no."

I thought about the rover situation we were all in because I had been convinced James had stolen our part.

"Everything will be okay," Johanna assured me. "She will get better."

I smiled at her, knowing she couldn't promise that. Nobody could. Sometimes things went wrong even when you read all the books and turned in the paperwork and knew all the rules.

Mallory appeared at the top of the stairs and rushed toward us, holding Orion, the rest of the bunkmates behind her. Meg was biting her nails.

"Leo called an emergency meeting in the robotics

lab," Mallory said, and Johanna and I popped up. It was obvious from the smile on Mallory's face that she didn't know why we were having a meeting. Charlotte looked like she was about to hyperventilate next to Ella.

Orion led the way like he did every morning, except nobody had trouble staying behind him. All of us trudged along, taking our time, dreading the sight of the RoboEngineers.

When we walked into the lab, Noah bounced out of his seat. "Cheaters! I saw you last night after lights-out! I saw you!"

And what could we say back? He was right.

I couldn't even look at James, sure he hated me more than anything.

"Sit," Leo said, and we sat at the table in the corner. "No, here." He pointed to the table next to the RoboEngineers', where they sat around their broken robot, parts scattered across the table. We shuffled over, trying hard not to make eye contact.

Leo sat in an empty chair on the RoboEngineers' side and I accidentally looked up and saw that James was slouched in his seat, not looking like the regular gloaty kind of James. In fact, he looked devastated.

"The RoboEngineers came in early this morning to work on their robot and were surprised to find that their robot was damaged."

"Ruined," Noah said, pushing his glasses up. "By them!"

Leo shushed him, pulling him back into his seat.

Mallory was standing behind me now, her arms crossed. "Do not tell me . . ." Orion was quiet at her feet, not even wagging or barking, like he was mad at us too.

"It was an accident," I said, allowing my eyes to flicker up at James. "We—I—thought you stole our motor module and when we went to look for it in your bin, we broke your robot." I looked up to see unforgiving faces. "I'm so sorry. From the bottom of my heart."

James held up a cracked sensor. "Accidentally? How could this be an accident? Did you 'accidentally' drop it from a thousand feet?"

I cleared my throat, shifting in my seat. "We stepped on it. We didn't mean to. It just . . . happened."

The RoboEngineers flung their hands around and made noises like they didn't believe me. Like my apology meant nothing.

James squinted his eyes at me. "Why would I want

to steal one of your parts? Did you see how awesome our robot was? We even programmed it with a little screwdriver to break into rocks."

Leo looked at us. "Accident or not, your team is responsible for this. It's very possible the RoboEngineers will not be able to recover before the competition tomorrow. How are you going to make it up to them?"

"Help them rebuild?" I said, but Noah stood up.

"We do not want your help," Noah said.

I looked at my team, but there was not much else we could offer. "You can take all of our bolts?"

The RoboEngineers turned around to look at the scores on the monitor.

"Four million bolts?" James said with a snort. "That will get us nowhere." They were still at zero from buying the gyro sensor and extra building sessions. And now they had basically spent all those bolts for nothing.

Leo picked up another one of their sensors. "The good thing is most of your sensors, except for one, are still in working order. I think you should take their bolts and buy another color sensor and start rebuilding. There isn't much time, but I think with an extra build session or two, you can do it."

James looked at his team miserably. "Fine."

"What about us?" Meg said. "Are we disqualified? Are you going to send us home?"

Leo looked at the RoboEngineers and Mallory and Alex. "I can't say we've ever had this kind of situation before. I think . . ."

Mallory bumped the back of my chair. "You snuck out to do this? Like, after lights-out?" It was almost a whisper, like our offense was so great, she couldn't even say it out loud.

I looked at the rest of the Red Rovers, who were studying their hands or closing their eyes like they couldn't bear what might come next. "Yes." I swallowed. "That was my idea too."

"You have a lot of really bad ideas!" Noah yelled.

I waited for Mallory to yell at me too, but she didn't, and that was almost worse.

"I should be the one sent home or disqualified," I said. "It's not their fault." I pointed to my teammates.

"You know," Alex said, coming to stand next to Mallory, "when you're an astronaut, the team is every-thing. If one person makes a bad decision, she takes the whole team with her."

How was I ever going to be the first girl on Mars if I couldn't even make it through Space Camp without messing up? Maybe I didn't have what it took to be an astronaut.

"I don't want to go home." Meg sniffled and my heart sank.

Leo sighed. "Well, we can't really send you home with just two days left of camp." He glanced at Mallory and Alex. "But sabotaging another team's robot is a serious offense and it deserves a serious penalty." He looked at me and the rest of my team. "We're going to have to disqualify the Red Rovers from the competition. All of your remaining bolts will be given to the RoboEngineers."

Ella choked in a breath next to me.

This was a nightmare.

CHAPTER 13

SAMUEL & BIRDY

Nobody really felt like eating lunch. Johanna didn't even get a second helping of macaroni and cheese. I kept my eyes on my bowl of fruit salad, my mind searching for ways to make all of this better. At the same time, the idea of Izzy, so sick in Chile, took my breath away and clouded my thoughts.

I pictured an echoey-quiet house without a little sister running around, and my lunch formed into a heavy ball in my stomach. It was hard, but I knew I had to stop thinking about Izzy and concentrate on the problem right in front of me, so I stood up with my lunch tray. It was time to talk to the guy with the robotic unicycle.

"Where are you going?" Johanna asked.

"I'm going to knock on the robotic-unicycle guy's door," I said, "and see if he has any sponsorships left. For the RoboEngineers."

"Good idea," Johanna said. "I'll go."

"Nope." I shook my head. "I got us into this mess and I'm going to fix it. I can do this on my own."

Nobody said anything, so I spun around and walked my tray of dirty dishes into the kitchen. When I got back, Charlotte stood up, stuffing the rest of her chocolate-chip cookie into her mouth. "I'm going too."

I shook my head.

"You heard what Alex said: The team is everything." Charlotte put her hands on her hips. "And we are all part of the same team, so we are going to do this together."

Ella stood up too. "Luci, stop taking all the blame for this. I'm the one who stepped on the robot. And Meg put the part in the wrong tub."

Meg nodded, wiping red sauce off her face.

"And we all snuck out," Johanna added.

"Without you we wouldn't even *be* a team. I hope you know that," Ella said, looking at the floor.

Charlotte grabbed Ella and gave her a strangling hug. "I'm so proud of you!" She pointed at me. "You are a good influence on her."

I laughed, a flicker of hope lighting in my heart. I couldn't believe what I was hearing. "Thanks, guys."

"So, now what?" Meg asked.

Johanna raised her fist. "We make socks!"

And then, together, we took the back way to the habitats, through the museum floor with the capsules that were actually used in space, past the moon rock on display, and over the floor pillows scattered around the common area.

"You go first because you are the bravest," Meg said to me, hiding behind Ella.

The door was in front of us now, tucked in the very back corner. A door that could have easily been missed by any Space Camper who wasn't looking for it.

"Director of Artificial Intelligence," Johanna read from the sign that hung on the doorknocker.

"Someone knock," Ella said.

Charlotte bit her nails. "Maybe we should just go, and there's a great chance that this person doesn't want guests otherwise—"

I knocked.

The rest of my team skittered away.

"Will you guys get over here!" I said, sending all sorts of threatening looks in their direction.

I straightened, hearing a shuffling from behind the

door. Johanna heard it too, and, being the good friend she was, she joined me, standing close. And then Ella stepped forward as well, Meg pulling Charlotte to stay back with her.

We could all hear the movement behind the door and also the sound of something else. Flapping? Chirping? And then the door flew open and a regular-looking guy stood there. Like, the kind of guy who you'd see walking down an everyday street instead of zipping around on a neon-lit robotic unicycle. Which is not that normal.

Except that he had a robotic bird on his shoulder. "SQUAWK! WHO GOES THERE, ME HEARTIES?"

The guy reached up and tapped the bird on his plastic head. "Sorry, he's in pirate mode right now."

"Oh, that's okay," I said because I didn't know what else to say. Johanna nudged me. "I'm Luciana Vega and these are my friends: Johanna, Ella"—I turned around, pointing—"and Charlotte and—"

Johanna tugged my shirt sleeve. "He's gone."

I peered through the door. "Uh, hello?"

As I poked my head in farther, I saw a giant office with a workbench, a couch, and some pictures on the wall. Not to mention there was also a dinosaur made entirely out of building bricks and beams that was so tall, it hit the ceiling. The bird was sitting on a perch by the window that looked out to the *Pathfinder*.

"Come in, come in." The guy waved, a handful of green beams in his hand. He was sitting in front of the giant mechanical dinosaur. "I've got to deliver this to the museum later today. Hand me that voice box?"

Johanna pushed past me and went in first. "Is this dinosaur Bluetooth enabled? Does it have . . ."

And then I didn't hear the rest because Meg screamed. I looked behind the door and saw a human-sized robot on a giant wheel with his eyes closed. Charlotte calmed down Meg and they walked inside.

"That's just Isaak," the guy said, pointing to the robot. "Another one of my projects."

Looking around the office, I realized we were surrounded by hundreds of projects, piled up on tables, pouring out of baskets, one stuck to the ceiling with suckers, another seemingly suspended in midair. In the corner by the couch that was covered in papers and parts was the robotic unicycle, plugged in and charging.

"Did you make the unicycle?" I asked, stepping over a pair of robot hands.

He looked up, taking a screwdriver out of his mouth. "I bought that one. I used it to figure out Isaak's wheel base." He motioned to Johanna to hand him a package of screws.

"Wow," Charlotte said, touching Isaak's shoulder with one finger. "I can't imagine what the programming was like for something like this."

"Veronica, what time is it?"

I looked around for a Veronica, and then I heard from the other side of the room, "Good afternoon, Samuel, it is one thirty-five." It came from a speaker hanging on the wall.

I stepped farther into the office. "Mr. Samuel? We are here because—"

"Quick, give me that washer." He waved his hand at Johanna, who handed him the part.

"Uh," I said, trying again. "We are the Red Rovers and—"

"Done! Watch this." He stepped off his stool and backed away, pressing his hands to his ears. We all quickly looked at one another and did the same thing. Which was a good idea because a second later, the dinosaur's voice box clicked on and released a roar loud enough to rattle the glasses lined up on the windowsill.

"Veronica. Send message 'He's ready' to Front Desk Lisa."

"Message sent," Veronica the speakerbot said.

I looked at the rest of my team, all now standing in the office, looking around in awe. This was the kind of place you'd expect a director of artificial intelligence to work for sure. But we were here for a reason. And that was to get a sponsorship.

"Mr. Samuel, we were wondering if you'd be willing to sponsor a team for the robotics com—"

"Help me get this on," he said, fighting to get a giant dinosaur leg onto a rolling platform. "And no, I don't sponsor anymore."

I froze. What? No more sponsorships? "But—"

"Wait! Wait! Don't pull!" he said to Johanna and Charlotte, who had moved in to help out.

Ella stood next to me.

"Now what?" I said.

She sighed. "Guess we'll have to get creative. Think of a different way to help the RoboEngineers."

I smiled at her because that was something she never would have said earlier in the week. She patted the glitter *L* that was rolling off a bit from my flight suit, fixing it back into place.

One of the dinosaur's scales had become detached from the rest of the dinosaur and slid to the floor. Johanna lunged to catch it before it shattered on the tile.

"Good catch!" Samuel said.

"Mr. Samuel?" Charlotte said, looking at the door behind her. "How are you going to get that dinosaur through the door?"

Samuel looked up from reattaching the scale. "Hmm. I always forget about that detail."

Everyone circled the dinosaur, including Meg, who walked fast past the humanoid behind the door.

Charlotte poked at one of the arm joints. "Looks like this could pop right off here. And also this one too. In fact, we could also take the head off."

Samuel cringed. "The head weighs at least fifty pounds and it took me three nights to build."

"That's it?" Meg said, stepping forward for a better look. "That would take me one thousand nights to build!"

"ONE THOUSAND NIGHTS TO BUILD," the robot bird said.

"Shhh," Samuel said. "Sleep, Birdy."

And the bird snoozed, snoring loudly.

"How many of these rolling platforms do you have?" Johanna pointed to the one under the dinosaur foot.

Samuel disappeared into a closet, coming back with more platforms and rolling them across the floor. "This many."

And that's how we ended up marching across Space Camp caravanning remote-controlled rolling platforms carrying a dismembered dinosaur.

CHAPTER 14

RAINBOW ROVER

Even though we were disqualified from the competition, Mallory and Alex still made us go to the robotics lab before dinner since it was our scheduled time. I wasn't sure exactly why they made us do this; maybe it was part of our punishment.

Nobody was surprised when the RoboEngineers grabbed their rover tub and went to build somewhere else, leaving us alone in the lab. They didn't want our help, and without the sponsorship, we had nothing to offer them anyway.

We were all just sitting there, not even really talking to one another, when Johanna pulled our plastic tub from the shelf. "Want to keep building anyway?" She took out our rover and placed it in the middle of the table.

"What's the point?" Ella said.

Meg reached over and pushed the rover back and forth. "It does look sad only half-finished."

"We could make it a really cool robot with lots of different parts," Charlotte said. "Just for fun."

Ella rolled her eyes. "We're disqualified, remember? Let's not waste our time."

Johanna sat down next to her, nudging her with an elbow. "Stop playing the insulted sausage."

I laughed. "Did you just call her a sausage?"

Johanna was up again, smiling and heading toward the parts wall. "It's just something we say in Germany, like . . ."

"Like, we should stop feeling sorry for ourselves?" I said.

"Yes! Like that!" Johanna waved us out of our seats. "Come on. We can just build something weird and fun."

"Hey, what can we do with these?" Charlotte asked, already in the parts closet, holding up four heavy-duty all-terrain wheels from a box. "They have spikes."

"Bring them here," Johanna said.

"Can we use this? I just found it in the trash can." Meg had an antennae-looking thing.

"Let's just try to use everything," Johanna suggested. "What do we have to lose?"

Charlotte came over and inspected the antennae. "I bet there's a remote that goes with this, or, oh wait, we could use the tablet to make it run."

Ella joined us. "Do both?" And then she looked at me like she was asking me the question.

I twirled my hair, the purple still vibrant after almost an entire week. "Yes. Both. Good." It was like Ella was finally treating me like a captain. And also a friend. And a teammate. "If you think so too," I added.

"What about these giant claws?" Meg said.

We started building. No drawings. No instructions. We just tried everything. The claws were too heavy for our motor module, so we took them off. But then Johanna found a set of pinchers that were just small enough.

And then Meg found an old voice-activated sensor with a giant scratch on the surface. "Think this still works?"

"Gimme," Charlotte said from her spot at the computer.

Meg brought it over and sat down next to Charlotte and then it was just Ella and me standing in the middle of the room while everyone else was busy building and programming.

"I can't believe tomorrow is the competition. And graduation is the next day," I announced. A week at Space Camp had seemed like it would be so long. I was ready to see Raelyn for sure, and I missed my parents, and I was desperate to find out what was happening with Izzy, but . . . A lump formed in my throat and I swallowed hard.

"I know," Ella said. "Do you think you'll come again?"

I shrugged. "I hope so. It took me a long time to win the essay contest, and with Izzy now, I'm just not sure."

"Yeah," Ella said.

I bit my nail. "Would you ever want to text or something? Like, keep in touch?" Even though Ella and I had a lot of differences, I felt that spark of friendship that you don't get with everyone.

"You want to keep in touch with me?" she said like she couldn't believe it. "I'm a terrible friend. You can ask anyone."

I laughed. "Well, I'm a terrible team captain, so we're even."

"Nah," Ella said, "you have some pretty good ideas." She tightened her ponytail.

I watched Charlotte and Johanna trying to connect the pinchers to the robot. "I probably won't take so many chances anymore. Slow down a little."

Ella shrugged. "It's not always bad to take chances. You're going to be a really great scientist. My dad is an inventor and he always says it's the person who thinks a little differently from the rest who has the greatest chance of making a difference in this world."

"Got it!" Johanna said. "Look! All-terrain walker!"

It was a walking rover but she had somehow rigged the all-terrain heavy-duty wheels to the end of the walking legs.

Charlotte squinted her eyes. "How am I supposed to program that? Do you want it to roll or walk?"

"Both!" Meg said, turning back to the computer. "You can do that, right, Charlotte?"

Charlotte nodded her head. "Whatever you say, glow sticks."

"Hey!" Meg stood up. "That would be so cool if we stuck glow sticks all over the robot. That way if it's dark, the astronauts could still see it. And, also, it would look awesome." She thought for a minute. "And some glitter stickers! Luciana, do you have some left?"

"Yep," I said. "Great idea, Meg."

"Oh, um." Ella sniffed, inspecting a strap on her flight suit. "Maybe you have some for me too?"

"Actually, maybe for all of us again?" Charlotte said.

"Of course!" I said, grinning.

Johanna stood up, pressing a button on the rover. "Watch." The rover moved his legs, but when she put it on the table to walk around, it collapsed. She scooped it up. "Okay. We need more thinking on this one obviously. Also, is there any duct tape in the lab?"

There was a knock on the door and we froze. Leo looked up from the drone he was fixing in the corner of the lab and motioned for me to open the door. I half expected it to be the boss of all of Space Camp coming to tell us our parents had been called and we were going home. But instead, it was James and his team.

"We're not here because we want to be," James said. "We have an emergency." He held out his robot. "The gyro sensor stopped working and we heard that one of you can fix almost anything."

Johanna stood up. "Let me look at it."

James hesitated for a second. "Without it we'd have

to redesign our entire robot. I think somehow it got damaged during the . . . uh—"

She pulled it out of his hands. "Give me a few minutes."

James hung onto his robot and looked over his shoulder. His teammates nodded at him, so he let it go.

Charlotte got to work on the gyro sensor with Johanna, and the rest of us stood around awkwardly, trying not to look at one another.

"You guys are building again?" James said, looking at our rover on the table.

"Just a little," I said. "For fun."

It was like we were in a robot hospital, waiting for news, until Johanna made a not-so-great sound and stood up. And from the look on Johanna's face, the news was not good.

"*Kaputt,*" she said.

"I think she means your sensor is dead," Charlotte whispered, and James smacked his head. The team moved around, standing up and sitting back down. Noah shook his head at me and I was pretty sure he mouthed *it's your fault*. It was okay, though, since he was right.

"Okay," I said. "This is what we're going to do." I

reached over to our robot and grabbed the voice-activated sensor. I held it up and looked at my team and we communicated via eyebrow signals. We all knew it was what we had to do.

"Here." I handed it to James. "We found it in a trash bin and fixed it up. It's probably the only one in the lab and it's not as great as the gyro sensor but it will make your team stand out."

James looked at me incredulously. "What are we supposed to do with this so late? The competition is tomorrow morning, Luciana. Tomorrow. The gyro sensor we paid ten million bolts for is busted and you want us to replace it with this?"

"I know," I said. "I'm so sorry. It's our best part. I just thought—"

He was steaming mad, pacing the room, half of his team joining him on his back-and-forths. "We'd have to completely reprogram and rebuild a new robot. Impossible."

I swung around and looked at my team. "Not if we all help."

James didn't look so sure, so he talked to his team and after a few seconds, he turned to me and gave me a thumbs-up.

We put aside our not-even-half-built robot and the RoboEngineers and Red Rovers sat at the same table and huddled over the broken robot. We pulled off sensors and arms and built more structure while Charlotte worked on the programming and Johanna messed with the voice-activated sensor. We worked for hours, barely even talking, until Mallory and Alex came into the room with trays full of food from the galley.

"Looks like you kids will be having what we call a working dinner," Alex said. "Reminds me of group projects in college. We had a lot of late nights."

Charlotte rushed over to the table, the programmed brick in her hand. "I think we got it." She clicked it into place and everyone stopped and waited, the room getting quiet.

"Can I do it?" Meg said.

Charlotte nodded. "Go for it."

"Rainbow Rover Roll."

The robot lit up, turning on and making a revving engine sound.

"Why Rainbow Rover?" James asked, standing up.

The voice activation sensor blinked alive, pulsing the color of the rainbow.

"Cool. Never mind. This is so cool."

Charlotte's face reddened and Meg did a half-turn twisty jump in the air because it looked like they'd got it. Rainbow Rover rolled.

"Rainbow Rover Drill."

Rainbow Rover pulled out one arm where a small drill was attached. The drill turned on, spinning as the robot rolled across the table.

"Rainbow Rover Stop," Charlotte said, and the robot stopped. She turned to everyone, like no big deal and she didn't just save the entire robot competition. "Okay, we can eat now."

And it was like the entire room had been holding their breath up until that point. Everyone grabbed some food from the trays and collapsed into chairs, even some of the boys smiling, everyone feeling a huge relief.

But then, out of the corner of my eye, I saw a guy on a robotic unicycle zipping up the hall toward the lab with a plastic bird on his shoulder. He poked his head in the door. "Pssst . . ."

Mallory and Alex waved to him. "Hey, Sammy. Hey, Birdy."

The bird on his shoulder said, "TWEET. I AM BIRDY, Y'ALL."

"Oh, a southern bird, I see." Mallory smiled and Orion woke up. "BARK."

I dropped my sandwich and walked over.

"Thanks for your team's help earlier," he said. "The dinosaur is safely installed in the museum now. I'd like to show you my appreciation by—" He pushed me aside and rolled into the room, directly over to our robot. "Did you make a robot out of broken parts?" He inspected the antenna that was being held together by duct tape.

"We kind of had to," Johanna said with her mouth full of mac and cheese. She pointed to the scoreboard where we were still at zero. The RoboEngineers were at three million after buying a few new parts to make up for some of their broken ones. The MarsBots were way ahead of everyone else, and the Wizards were close behind them.

"I love this idea. Whose idea was this?" Samuel asked, looking around and picking up our robot's pincher at the same time. "Recycled robot. Genius."

My entire team was pointing at me and my heart throbbed. "Johanna did all the fixing and Ella did a lot of the building. Charlotte and Meg were the programmers."

"And you," he said, pointing at me, "were the idea generator."

"Well, I don't always have the best ideas."

The boys were all out of their chairs by now, hovering around, looking at Samuel's unicycle.

Samuel handed me a ticket. "I haven't sponsored a team in a long time, you know."

The rest of my team crowded in to see. The ticket was for ten million bolts. More than any sponsorship we had seen all week. I glanced up at Mallory. She gave me a thumbs-up.

"Oh, but—" I started to say, also looking at the rest of my team. "We didn't want the bolts for ourselves."

Samuel glanced up from our robot. "What?"

"We were hoping you'd sponsor a different team." I nodded toward James and his team. "One that really deserves it. Plus, we're disqualified, so the bolts would only go to waste."

Samuel was surprised.

James stood up. "Luciana, wait . . ."

"We owe the RoboEngineers big-time for messing things up for them," I said.

"Like bigger than big-time," Charlotte said.

Johanna nodded and so did Ella, even though her

eyes were fixated on the ten-million-bolt ticket like she would snatch it back if things were different.

"Like the biggest of the big-times ever," Meg added.

"You want to give your ten million bolts to another team?" Samuel said, rocking back and forth on his unicycle.

"Yes," I said, and Ella handed the ticket over to James, who only just stared at it.

"Guys . . ." James said. "It's okay. We're okay now. You helped us."

Ella took the ticket back. "All right, since you don't want it, and we can't use it . . . Here you go, Mr. Samuel."

"No!" Noah launched himself from his table, half a turkey sandwich still in his grip. "I mean, please don't throw it away," he said, straightening his glasses. "We'll take it. Don't be silly."

James smiled at me. "Thank you. I can't believe you'd do this for us. Thank you."

Samuel's walkie-talkie buzzed and he put it to his ear. "This is Sammy."

And we heard, "Come and turn down this dinosaur racket; he's about to wreck all of our eardrums!" through the speaker.

"Yes, ma'am," he said back. "Be there in a minute.

"Sounds like they need me at the museum," he said to us, heading out of the lab.

We all waved and thanked him for coming and said we hoped we'd see him at the competition the next morning.

He stopped at the door. "Also, thanks for knocking on my door today. I haven't been in the robotics lab for a long time. It was nice coming back."

And then he zoomed off in a blur of neon lights, Birdy squawking, "SEE YOU LATER, Y'ALL."

CHAPTER 15

THE COMPETITION

We ate breakfast on the go the next morning, heading straight to the robotics competition under the *Pathfinder* with our bagels and muffins and bananas. It was cool outside, with a quiet breeze running under the rocket boosters. We sat on the grass, beside the rows of chairs set up in a circle around the robot arena, the competition table in the center of it all.

James ran up to us. "Go get your rover," he said, out of breath.

"What?" I jumped up. "Why?"

"Leo said you can do the competition. I mean, not officially. You can't win, but you can still take your turn."

"Why would he say that?" Charlotte said. We all looked at one another, confused.

James looked at the ground. "Our team just thought that you built a really cool robot, and after you helped us so much, we asked the crew trainers if you could do the competition today."

Johanna popped up, clapping. "I'll go get him." And she raced off toward the building.

I grinned, looking at the rest of our team. "That was really nice of you, James."

"It's nothing," James said. "We just thought people should see what you built." He started walking backward away from us to where his team sat with their robot under a shady tree.

Ella, Meg, and Charlotte stood next to me now. "Well, thank you!" I called after him. "And good luck!"

When Johanna got back, we sat down to finish our breakfast, our rover in the grass in front of us. We had named him Mohawk because of his spiky mohawk of glow sticks.

"I love the all-terrain tires," I said.

"And the antennae," Ella said.

"It would have been so cool if it was voice-activated," Charlotte said. "Not that I'm not happy for the RoboEngineers, but . . ."

Johanna swallowed her bite of blueberry muffin. "But we have this guy." She pushed a button on top of the robot and a little box in its rear opened up and out popped a telescoping propeller.

"How did you make that? So genius, Johanna." I touched one of the propellers, which was made out of a bunch of building bricks.

"It would never fly, obviously," Johanna said, her mouth full.

"But it's such a good idea because if the terrain is super rocky and the wheels don't work or if the robot gets to a little mountain, he can open up the propeller and fly over it," Charlotte said.

"It's a walking, rolling, flying rover." Ella smiled at me. "Brilliant."

One of her glitter letter *L*s was peeling off her flight suit a bit, so I reached over and pushed the edge back down. She had chosen all pink letters, not the color I would have expected from Ella. But then again, I was finding people were full of surprises all over the place.

"We should have given it flippers to swim too," Charlotte said.

And then our walking, rolling, flying rover toppled over from the weight of the propeller.

Johanna shook her head. "Rookie mistake." And we laughed.

"I'm glad, though, that James's robot is all fixed," Ella said after we were all quiet.

We took our places in the chairs just as the rest of Space Camp was arriving to watch the big competition, with Mohawk getting a chair of his own between Johanna and Ella. Even though our rover wasn't in the running to win, I still felt the familiar tug of nerves in my belly. Maybe because the robot competition pretty much meant the end of Space Camp. And maybe I wasn't ready to leave for home just yet. I twirled my purple streak between my fingers. Raelyn and I would be back together soon. But what about Johanna, Charlotte, Ella, and Meg? I'd have rainbow hair if I dyed a streak of color for each one of them.

Ella bumped me with her shoulder and smiled like she knew what I was thinking. I bumped her back.

"Welcome to the Space Camp Robotics Competition!" Leo announced, and everyone took their seats, teams and their rovers crowding around the arena area. When I turned around, I saw James and his team on the grass making last-minute adjustments to Rainbow Rover. I waved and he waved back.

"We have five teams competing for the Best Rover at Space Camp Award," Leo said, "and from what I've seen over our week together in the lab, this is going to be a tough and close competition."

The teams were squeezing in toward the front now, taking seats and rolling their rovers under the rocket boosters. I noticed nobody else had a walking rover, or a flying one, for that matter.

"Each team will get a chance to run their rover through the competition course. Your rover will be responsible for taking a Martian rock sample and sending it into orbit for pickup within these four stations." He pointed to each of the different areas of the table. "Each station your robot completes will be ten million bolts for your team, but each minute will cost you one million." Behind him was the monitor from the lab with all the scores. The RoboEngineers were in the lead, thanks to Mr. Samuel, with thirteen million bolts. The MarsBots and Space Heroes were close behind with eleven million, followed by the Ninja Coders with nine million bolts. The Wizards only had five million bolts, and even though we had been disqualified, we were still listed in last place with zero. "The team with the most bolts at the end wins."

Mallory and Alex sat in the front row with Orion and then it was time for the competition to begin. The first two teams were just okay and didn't score a lot of points. I shot a look to James, who smiled at me. Mostly they had very basic rovers that came straight from the lab challenges throughout the week. One of them had trouble with its color sensor and picked up all blue rocks instead of red; another team used a hammer to smash their samples and balls flew everywhere off the table; and neither of the robots could make it up the sandy and rocky surface of Regolith Mountain.

But then it was the MarsBots' turn. Their rover had no problem with station one or two, but then had to chase the rolling rocks around station three for a few minutes before it was able to keep one still enough to get a rock sample. They used a pick connected to a jointed robot arm to break into the red ball and a set of pinchers to retrieve the sample. Everyone cheered when the robot held up the small piece of rock. A pick was a great idea. When their rover got to the bottom of Regolith Mountain, it took a minute to move all of its sampling arms to the front and then it slowly climbed the rocky terrain. And the extra weight in the front must have helped, because it was the first rover in the competition to make it all the way up and hit the elevator button. In the end, their score was thirty-six million bolts, and when that was added to the bolts they already had, they had a total of forty-seven million bolts.

Then it was our turn. We stood up, our giant duct-taped robot tucked under Johanna's arm, and placed it into the starting position. Charlotte and Meg turned it on from their tablet, its little robot engine making engine noises, its spiky mohawk glowing in the shade of the rocket boosters. We stood together, all of us in our official Space Camp flight suits with not-so-official glitter-sticker names above our pockets and watched as our rover walked on his all-terrain wheels. With a little more time, we had hoped to program Mohawk to roll on his wheels too. He would have been a rover for all environments, but we'd spent our time doing the right thing by helping James and his team. And there was no better feeling than when you did the right thing.

Mohawk didn't do great at collecting the rocks, and he did even worse trying to get up the sandy and rocky hill. His legs were too short and since his wheels didn't work, he got stuck. Charlotte and Meg opened up his propeller and it unfolded in front of everyone's eyes. We heard murmurs of surprise and we all grinned at one another. But then, as expected, Mohawk fell over on his side and our run was over.

Meg picked him up and dusted him off and we returned to our seats. Mallory gave us a thumbs-up, and even Alex did too.

The Space Heroes were up next, and as soon as they put their robot at the starting position, we all looked at one another. Their robot was compact with two sampling arms on its top, one with a basket scoop and the other a sharp-looking pincher. Maybe if someone didn't know robots a lot, they'd think the Space Heroes didn't know what they were doing with such a small creation. But we did. And so did James by the look on his face. Their robot looked fast and sturdy and light. Three of the best qualities of a Space Camp robot, according to Leo.

The timer started and the robot was off, easily identifying the right rocks and collecting them in station two. We were all holding our breaths. Johanna grabbed my hand. The robot lowered its basket scoop with the sample and tried cracking the rock open with its pinchers. But the rock bounced out of the basket scoop and they had to start again. The team looked flustered, and on their second try, they pushed the rock against the wall to keep it from bouncing out of the basket, but the judges shook their heads at them. That wasn't allowed. So they tried crushing the rock with its pinchers. The little yellow sample ball popped out and they were able to catch it with their scooper, the team taking a giant breath of relief. And then they easily climbed Regolith Mountain and sent their sample into orbit. Their time was two minutes thirty-seven seconds. The fastest time by far. They earned thirty-eight million bolts, and when added to the eleven million they already had, the Space Heroes were in the lead with forty-nine million bolts.

When it was the RoboEngineers' turn, our team could barely watch. We covered our faces when they got to the rock-sampling part. I looked at Charlotte, hoping she had programmed the screwdriver just right. If she had, the rock should split apart effortlessly. But nobody had thought about holding the rock in place. Nobody had even considered that to be a problem. Not until now, at least. But James and his team looked calm and confident. They knew the rock sampling was going to be more difficult than they had anticipated. James turned on the screwdriver, which buzzed through the quiet crowd. The first time the screwdriver came down on the rock, the rock skittered away. The second time, James first put the screwdriver on the rock and then turned it on. The rock flew to the side, banging against the plastic arena fence. James wiped his forehead. The third time, the robot brought the screwdriver down hard on the rock like a hammer, embedding the sharp tip in the rock. When James turned the screwdriver on, the rock broke apart easily.

After the robot sent their sample up the space elevator, the timer read three minutes fifteen seconds. Nearly a minute longer than the Space Heroes. I couldn't watch the scoreboard, afraid that the news wouldn't be good. If their gyroscope hadn't been busted, would they have been faster? Johanna nudged me and I looked up. The RoboEngineers got a score of thirty-seven million bolts, and added to the thirteen million bolts they already had thanks to Mr. Samuel, they had a final score of fifty million. The RoboEngineers had won.

CHAPTER 16

GRADUATION

After breakfast the next morning, we headed into the gift shop, our last stop before graduation, and it looked like almost everyone had had the same idea as us. James and some of the boys headed to the rockets, Johanna found the only tool kit in the place, and Charlotte and Meg drooled over the programmable robots that cost more than a Space Camp tuition.

What caught my eye weren't the robots for sale or the art kits or the how-to-draw-a-Mars-rover books, but the necklaces hanging from a display by the counter. Home rushing back to me. My parents. Isadora.

I held my star necklace and looked at the sun and comet and constellation charms on sparkly silver chains. And it wasn't until I'd pretty much studied each and every necklace on the spinner that I spotted one that had a different charm than the rest. A moon, full and shiny bright, with a second charm hanging over the top. A little glittering blue gem.

"For baby Isadora?" Johanna stood next to me, her Space Camp toolbox under her arm.

I nodded my head. Because now that the robot competition was over, it was all I could think about. A little sister. Maybe. For me.

Graduation was under the *Pathfinder* in the shuttle park, and after we made our purchases, we walked over together, the Red Rovers, the RoboEngineers, Alex, and Mallory. Orion buzzed out ahead of us, his alarms going off because the ceremony was about to start. We took seats as close to the front row as possible, all of us looking at the family section to see if our parents were there.

One by one teams got called up to the front with their crew trainers, marching up to the little stage wearing their blue flight suits and looking like professional kids who might become astronauts one day. Mostly everyone was given a graduation certificate and a patch for their flight suit, but every once in a while, someone got a special medal. One kid with a spiky mohawk got a Most Creative medal. My team looked at me like that should have been my medal or something, but after our late-night romp to the robotics lab, I knew there would be no medals for me.

When Team Odyssey was called, Orion led the way of course, and we all lined up in front of the rest of camp and all the parents and families. I looked again for my parents, squinting past the glare of sunlight on the underbelly of the *Pathfinder*, but I didn't see them. Ella, Charlotte, and Meg's family, on the other hand, were standing up and waving and also picking up all the chairs Ella's brothers knocked over by accident. I saw Ella shake her head, but I also saw her smile.

Alex and Mallory took the microphone first and said a lot of nice things about our team and how even though we hit some bumps in the road, in the end, we worked better together than any team they'd had in the past.

"We're proud of you," they said, and the audience clapped, and we all looked at one another trying to figure out if we should clap too.

I couldn't stop looking for my parents, feeling my heart skipping a bit each time I saw a mom wearing sunglasses on her head, something my mom always did. And, if I was being honest, I wasn't sure I wanted to see them while I was up here onstage in front of everyone. Because I'd know in a flat second if there were any updates on Izzy. And I'd know if they had been the good kind of updates or not. Just by the looks on their faces.

When Leo stepped up, Johanna and Ella nudged me. It was time for the RoboEngineers to get their award.

Leo cleared his throat into the microphone. "Best Rover is what every Space Camp robotics camper strives for. This week, our competition was fierce. There were a lot of great ideas and a lot of hard work. I'm proud to give the Best Rover Award to the RoboEngineers with a final score of fifty million bolts, a near record for this camp."

Everyone clapped and Leo stepped in front of the RoboEngineers and handed them each a patch for their flight suits. James held his up for me to see. It was embroidered with a *Curiosity* rover and in bright red it said "Best Rover" above the Space Camp logo. I gave him a thumbs-up. It was a cool patch and it would look even cooler when he sewed it onto his flight suit.

And then from way back in the audience we heard a loud "WHOOP WHOOP!" It was Samuel and Birdy on their robotic unicycle, zooming up to the stage. Ella and I looked at each other.

Samuel patted Birdy's head when he got to us. "I'm working on his party-bird mode."

"PARTY TIME!" Birdy said.

"Let me introduce you to our director of artificial intelligence, Samuel, and his robotic bird, Birdy," Leo said into the microphone, handing it off to Samuel after he parked his unicycle on the side of the stage.

"Whoa, there are a lot of you," Samuel said with a nervous laugh, looking out at the audience. "Uh, so, a while back when I was a crew trainer here, I used to give out a special award for teams that took a big risk and followed through on an idea even if it meant it might fail in the end."

I perked up, looking over my shoulder at Samuel and Birdy.

"It's not a bad thing. Failing is an important part of advancing science. Crucial, even." He rummaged in his pocket, pulling out a Space Camp patch. "It's called the Fail Smart and it's been a few years since I've given one out, but I met a team this year that really deserves this award."

My face started to burn, and I felt Johanna move closer to me. "HOORAY!" Birdy said.

"The Red Rovers were disqualified from the robotics competition"—he looked at us meaningfully and I stared at the floor of the stage—"but instead of sitting back, they got together and built a rover made entirely out of junk parts. Even though they couldn't officially enter into the competition and even though they knew they wouldn't have enough time to make it run perfectly, they still gave it a try. They took a risk even though they knew they might fail. So, for that reason I'd like to bring the Fail Smart Award out of retirement. Congratulations, Red Rovers." Samuel gave the microphone back to Mallory and handed us each a Fail Smart patch, and then he leaned over and gave me a big hug.

"You have a gift, Luciana," he whispered. "Don't ever forget it."

"HAPPY BIRTHDAY, DEAR BIRDY!" Birdy squawked, nearly breaking my eardrum.

We laughed and Orion started barking and Birdy started singing a song about jolly good fellows and I was relieved when Mallory and Alex led us off the stage because I couldn't stop wiping my eyes.

CHAPTER 17

REACHING FOR THE STARS

After graduation, it was time to find our families, but we all moved slowly from our seats until Mallory and Alex finally told us to stop stalling. That good-byes were not forever and they hoped to see us back at Space Camp someday. So we gave hugs and handshakes and even Noah gave me a fist bump. "No bad feelings?" I said.

He thought about it. "You have some really bad ideas, like the worst I ever saw, but okay." He smiled at me.

We heard a yipping and a moment later Pepper busted through the crowd of adults and kids standing around the shuttle park. Meg lunged forward, catching him. "Peppy! Peppy!" she said, falling to the ground with the squiggly dog, who was pouncing all over her, licking and snuffling.

Ella and Charlotte joined Meg on the grass and Pepper ran circles around the three of them. And a second later, the rest of their family poured through, sunburned, chomping gum, carrying kids and babies, and helping a gray-haired lady push her walker through the thick grass.

And then they were doing the group family hug again and I made Johanna join it with me. Because a week of walking on the moon, piloting spacecraft, and surviving the Multi-Axis Trainer together made us all more than just regular friends. More like a family, right?

The hug broke up and someone had to run after Pepper when he skittered toward the museum entrance and someone else had to run after one of the babies headed for the parking lot.

James walked up to us. "Thanks again for helping us yesterday and also for giving us your sponsorship. You didn't have to do that."

"Yes, we did," I said. "We ruined your rover."

"Well, I'm just saying thank you, that's all. Because of you and your team, our robot won."

"Well, we did all work well together," I acknowledged.

"Maybe if you ever come back to Space Camp, we could try to come the same week again?" James asked.

I nearly choked I was so surprised. After all that we did?

"Deal," I said, holding out my hand to shake.

James found the rest of my teammates, and shook their hands too. And then he turned around, gave a final wave, and joined the RoboEngineers standing under one of the rocket boosters.

Charlotte and Ella and Meg had to leave when one of the brothers ran into a trash can and tipped it over with a giant bang onto the concrete sidewalk. We hugged and hugged again and promised to call and write. And just as Ella was walking away, she showed me what she bought at the gift shop.

"I think you're right." She shrugged. "It's worth a try."

It was a postcard.

"Best friends are always worth another try," I said.

She held up a bunch more. "I got a few extra for some new friends." She grinned, and ran to catch up with her family.

And then it was just me, Johanna, and Mallory, waiting for my parents to come. "Samuel was right, you know," Mallory said. "You girls amazed me this week.

First, I was shocked at how you broke the rules and ruined another team's robot. But then, I was also amazed at how you found a sponsor to help another team. How you were able to work together and build a really cool robot. Most kids would probably have given up. But not your team. Not with you as captain.

"You're going to be a great big sister," she said, squeezing my shoulder, before running off to get Orion, who was zooming across the shuttle park.

And that's when I saw my parents walking through the grass to reach me. "Mom! Dad!" I ran to meet them and pulled them back with me to meet Johanna. She was coming to the airport with us and I was thankful to have a few more minutes with her before saying good-byes. Saying good-bye to friends was not my specialty.

"Congratulations," Mom and Dad said, each bending down to give me a kiss.

"But what was all that about being disqualified?" Dad asked with a bit of a frown.

I felt my face growing hot. I knew I had to come clean. "I'll explain it all on the way home," I told them. "But first, I have to show you something," I said, reaching into my pocket.

I held up the necklace and it glittered in the sun, the light hitting the gem in just the right place.

"Beautiful," Mom said. "Is this what you bought with your spending money? A necklace to go with your star necklace?"

"They will look so nice together," Dad said.

I put the necklace on. "I bought it for Isadora." I couldn't look at them. Johanna put her arm over my shoulder. My gift was silly, because why buy a necklace for a sister I might never have? But somehow it just seemed right.

Mom and Dad looked at each other and for a minute, my heart was simultaneously leaping and sinking, because I had never seen that look before. Was it a good look or a bad look? What were they not telling me?

Johanna must have seen it too because she squeezed my hand.

"Abuelita found Isadora at the hospital, Luciana." Dad reached into his wallet. "And she sent us this."

My heart leapt. Dad held up a picture of a baby girl playing with a stuffed penguin on a blanket in the grass. Tubes came out of her little dress and pressed into her nose.

"Is she okay?" I asked, my heart sinking again, seeing all those tubes. I clutched my necklaces.

Mom nodded. "Izzy has a heart condition." She looked at Dad. "It's quite serious." Johanna squeezed my hand harder. "They're going to push our paperwork through in hopes she can come home and get her treatment here."

It took a minute to sink in. "So." I looked at Johanna, hardly believing. "Then she's going to be my sister?"

Mom and Dad smiled. "You are going to be a big sister, Luci."

That was amazing news. I grabbed Johanna and hugged her, and then I took the picture of Izzy and held it close to my chest, resting it against the necklaces.

"That's your copy," Mom whispered to me. "Dad printed off about five hundred."

We followed my parents to the car, Johanna linking my elbow so I could stare at my picture some more. And then I noticed Isadora was reaching her little hands out, up to the sky.

That's when I knew she was just like me. She was already reaching for the stars.

ABOUT THE AUTHOR

Erin Teagan is the author of *The Friendship Experiment* and worked in science for more than ten years before becoming a writer. She uses many of her experiences from the lab in her books and loves sharing the best and most interesting (and most dangerous and disgusting) parts of science with kids. Erin lives in Virginia with her family, a ninety-pound lapdog, and a bunny that thinks he's a cat. Visit her at www.erinteagan.com

AUTHOR'S NOTE

To write *Luciana*, Erin went to the real Space Camp®
at the U.S. Space & Rocket Center in Huntsville,
Alabama, where she rode the Multi-Axis Trainer,
commanded a virtual shuttle launch, visited the
robotics lab, went on a simulated mission to Mars,
and even scuba dived in the underwater astronaut
trainer. Although this book was inspired by Erin's
experience at camp, liberties were taken in writing
Luciana's story. When kids go to the real Space Camp
in Alabama, Robotics and Space Camp are separate
programs. And at Space Camp, their top priority is
the safety and security of their trainees. Unlike in the
story, children are supervised at all times.

SPECIAL THANKS

With gratitude to Dr. Deborah Barnhart, CEO, and
Pat Ammons, director of communications at the U.S.
Space & Rocket Center, for guiding Luciana's journey
through the extraordinary world of Space Camp;
astronaut Dr. Megan McArthur; Dr. Ellen Stofan,
former chief scientist at NASA; Maureen O'Brien,
manager of strategic alliances at NASA; and the rest
of the NASA Headquarters and Johnson Space
Center teams, for their insights and knowledge
of space exploration.

READY TO REACH
FOR THE STARS
WITH
Luciana ?

VISIT
americangirl.com to learn more about
Luciana's world!

Meet Gabriela McBride™

When the city threatens to close her beloved community arts center, Gabriela is determined to find a way to help. Can she harness the power of her words and rally her community to save Liberty Arts?

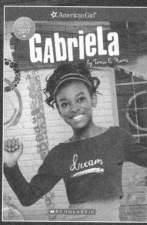

Meet TENNEY Grant™

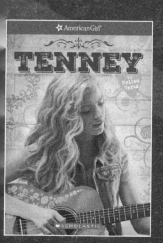

Her biggest dream is to share what's in her heart through music. Little does she know, she's about to get the opportunity of a lifetime.

★ American Girl®

📖 SCHOLASTIC

A group of girls so close, they're just

Like Sisters

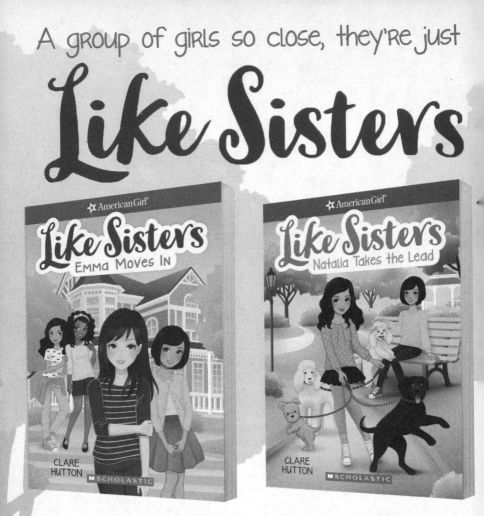

Emma loves visiting her twin cousins, Natalia and Zoe, so she's thrilled when her family moves to their town after living 3,000 miles away. Emma knows her life is about to change in a big way. And it will be more wonderful and challenging than any of the girls expect!

Several dogs are staying with their owners at the family's B&B. Natalia eagerly volunteers to watch and walk all of them with the help of her sister Zoe and her cousin Emma. But Zoe and Emma have their own commitments, and Natalia is quickly overwhelmed. When one of the dogs goes missing, will Natalia be able to step up and make things right?

AGLIKESISTERS